Reading
Philip Larkin:
Selected Poems

John Gilroy

Literature Insights
General Editor: Charles Moseley

Reading Philip Larkin: Selected Poems

John Gilroy

$\mathcal{HEB}$ ☼ Humanities-Ebooks, LLP

COPYRIGHT

First published by *Humanities-Ebooks, LLP,*
Tirril Hall, Tirril, Penrith CA10 2JE

ISBN 978-1-84760-100-1 PDF
ISBN 978-1-84760-202-2 Paper

Contents

Acknowledgements & Abbreviations

The images of Larkin from Hull University Archives are reproduced by kind permission of the University of Hull, who own the copyright.

The author would like to thank Dr C. W. R. D. Moseley for his editorial suggestions and Emily Gilroy-Martin for help and advice.

Abbreviations

CP: Thwaite, Anthony, ed., *Philip Larkin: Collected Poems* (London: Faber, 1988).

EPJ: Tolley, A. T. ed., *Philip Larkin: Early Poems and Juvenilia* (London: Faber, 2005).

FR: Thwaite, Anthony, ed., *Philip Larkin: Further Requirements* (London: Faber, 2001).

SL: Thwaite, Anthony, ed., *Selected Letters of Philip Larkin:1940– 1985* (London: Faber, 1992).

Motion: Motion, Andrew, *Philip Larkin: A Writer's Life* (London: Faber, 1993).

RW: Philip Larkin: *Required Writing: Miscellaneous Pieces 1955– 1982* (London: Faber, 1983).

Part 1: Life and Times

1.1 Early Life and Schooldays

It is March 1946 and the twenty-four year old Larkin writes a letter to his long-term friend, Jim Sutton, full of his sense of the joy of life. A flawless, early Spring day has put him into the best of moods—like listening to Earl Hines, he says, 'after a YMCA piano-basher' (*SL* 114). He goes on to say how privileged he feels to be able to walk about on such a day and how it 'makes nonsense temporarily of all one's hopes and fears'. With a possible allusion to Pope's, 'life can little more supply / Than just to look about us, and to die,'[1] Larkin advises Sutton,

Larkin in August 1960
© The University of Hull

> 'All that matters is that we've got only fifty years, at the outside, to look around. So let us be as eager and meticulous as a Boston Vice Squad on a mixed bathing-beach, and if we should produce art, so much the better, but the only quality that makes art durable and famous is the quality of generating delight in the state of living' (*SL* 115).

This early letter is very characteristic of Larkin. First of all, there is his obvious love of life, a simple, physical responsiveness to the

---

1   *Essay on Man*: Epistle 1, ll.3–4.

world in which he finds himself. There is the hint of his already well-established enthusiasm for jazz music, as well as his use of slightly sardonic humour in the well-chosen vice-squad analogy. But overridingly we discover the purposive seriousness that makes him ambitious not only to be a writer who is accessible and enjoyable but also one whose work will be 'durable and famous'. It is interesting, however, that the lovely Spring weather makes a nonsense only 'temporarily' of his hopes and fears. All Larkin's enjoyments must compete with his all-pervading sense of the brevity of existence. Even at the age of twenty-one he was writing in his first novel, *Jill*, 'see how little anything matters. All that anyone has is the life that keeps him going, and see how easily that can be patted out. See how appallingly little life is'. Life is brief at the longest and Larkin is never able to rid himself of a morbid disquiet that 'Whether or not we use it, it goes'.[1] In some ways it is true to say that for Larkin, as for a poet like John Donne, for example, the whole of his life was a preparation for his taking leave of it. In fact Steve Clark sees his 'unsparing meditation on ageing, death, "endless extinction,"' as aspiring to what he calls 'a kind of agnostic sainthood'.[2]

Philip Larkin was born in Coventry in 1922. His father, Sydney, who became Treasurer for Coventry City Council was a not unkind but distinctly authoritarian figure in a household which included Larkin's self-effacing mother, Eva, and his elder sister, Catherine (known as 'Kitty'). Sydney had a powerful influence on Larkin. Throughout the thirties he was a sympathiser with the resurgent Germany under the National Socialists, and took his teenage son there on two separate visits in 1936 and 1937. Apart from a few days in Paris in 1952 and a brief trip to Hamburg to receive a prize in 1976, Larkin would never again venture further 'abroad' than Ireland and the Channel Isles. Within the sober atmosphere Sydney Larkin created around his family he ensured that Philip was given a good grounding in the literature he himself particularly admired. This included the solidly respectable works of nineteenth and twentieth-century writers—such

---

1   'Dockery and Son', l.46.
2   Clark, Steve, '"Get out as early as you can": Larkin's Sexual Politics' in Hartley, George, *Philip Larkin 1922-1985: A Tribute* (London: The Marvell Press, 1988) p.238.

people as Hardy, Arnold Bennett, Christina Rossetti, Housman, but also the Modernist novelists Joyce and Lawrence, the poets T. S. Eliot and Ezra Pound, as well as the new left-wing writers of the thirties such as Isherwood, Spender, Auden. Larkin's work would go on to reflect a whole range of such influences and it is clear that Sydney Larkin was a crucial figure, not only in the formation of his son's literary tastes but also in the encouragement he gave to him in his other interests such as jazz music.[1]

Larkin's schooldays were conventionally happy ones. At junior school he made friends with James (Jim) Sutton with whom, during the most formative period of his life, he would carry on a correspondence for twenty or so years. Later, as a senior pupil at King Henry VIII School, Coventry, he added two more lifelong friends, Colin Gunner and Noel (Josh) Hughes. The different temperaments of these schoolfellows appealed to various aspects of his own make up. With Sutton he shared the profounder, cultural, interests of literature, music and art, while Hughes and Gunner reflected his more outgoing self. It is fair to say that Larkin's popular reputation has never been remarkable for anything more than unalleviated gloom and pessimism.[2] In fact, this is a major misrepresentation. From his school and university days and throughout his professional career to the end of his life, friends, colleagues, correspondents and acquaintances testify to his highly developed sense of humour, which suggests a penetrating intelligence and an ability to recognise, as well as the larger tragedies of existence, the comedy in daily routines. It is not surprising that one of the things for which he gives a 'Hurray' is 'hearing Al Read' while on holiday in the Western Isles of Scotland in 1971.[3] Al Read was a popular radio comedian who based his humour on his own observations of the quirks and foibles of common life. In interview Larkin expresses his own general love of the commonplace and how he doesn't want to transcend it. 'I lead a very commonplace life,'

---

1   Sydney subscribed his son to a jazz magazine, *Down Beat*, and bought him a drum kit.
2   An image Larkin was happy to play up to: 'Gloomy old sod, aren't I[...]' concludes a letter to Judy Egerton, *SL* 503, and ironically of himself to John Wain, 'What I like about Phil, he always cheers you up' (*SL* 710).
3   Quoted in Motion, p. 414.

he says, 'Everyday things are lovely to me' (*FR* 57).

While as a schoolboy he was pursuing a fairly unremarkable academic career, beneath the surface appearance of the bespectacled student with a slight stammer was another Larkin acquainting himself with the subversive jazz music of black America, as well as developing talents for art and caricature and trying his hand at writing fiction and poetry of his own. Larkin's earliest poems appeared in his school magazine, *The Coventrian*, and, although derivative, they reveal a genuine talent for form, music and rhythm. Essentially, though, his ambition was to be a novelist and his creative energy at this time went much more into the production of prose fiction than of poetry. In his recollection of these early years in Coventry, 'Not the Place's Fault',[1] he talks of how he 'wrote ceaselessly [...] now verse, which I sewed up into little books, now prose, a thousand words a night after homework'. Such activity suggests real earnestness and self-scrutiny, but predominantly an ambition to leave his mark on the literary world. This youthful confidence in his ability can perhaps sometimes masquerade as egotism, as when later, in a letter to Sutton he remarks, 'I was not meant to study, but to be studied,'[2] but has more in common with Wordsworth's paradoxical term, 'proud humility'. He could be equally self-deprecatory as in a letter to Monica Jones in 1966 where, in admitting to holding off everything in order to write, he adds, 'Anyone wd think I was Tolstoy, the value I put on it. It hasn't amounted to much' (*SL* 387).

In 1938 Larkin took his Lower School Certificate examinations and, although he did not especially distinguish himself, the combined opinions of his Headmaster and English master, who recognised his potential, allowed him to continue to Sixth Form studies, whence he proceeded to read English at St John's College, Oxford, having gained a distinction in the subject in his Higher School Certificate.

---

1   'Not The Place's Fault', in Chambers, Harry, ed., *An Enormous Yes: In Memoriam Philip Larkin (1922-1985)* (Calstock: Peterloo Press, 1986) pp. 48-53.
2   Quoted in Motion, p.103.

1.2 Oxford and after

Oxford provided Larkin with real opportunity to develop his gifts and he immediately entered into the spirit of undergraduate life, dressing in colourful trousers, wearing bow ties and generally living out the part of the young poet. In fact he had arrived at Oxford an already published poet, as a poem in the style of Auden called 'Ultimatum' had been selected to appear from among four he had submitted to *The Listener* in June 1940. His two school friends were also at Oxford: Noel Hughes like himself at St John's, and Jim Sutton who had been transferred from London with the Slade School of Art for the duration of the war. The conflict with Germany had disrupted undergraduate life for many of Larkin's contemporaries, but he himself was able to complete his three year degree course without interruption as an army medical examination in January 1942 found that his poor eyesight had made him unfit for military service. Larkin also established new friendships at Oxford with, among others, Norman Iles, a figure who, like his extrovert friend Colin Gunner, appealed to the subversive element in his temperament, and Bruce Montgomery, a talented and worldly young man who composed and played music as well as going on to write detective fiction under the name 'Edmund Crispin'. But by far the most important friendship which began at this time was with Kingsley Amis who first appeared at Oxford in the Summer of Larkin's first term there. Amis of course would go on to become one of the late twentieth-century's most significant popular novelists and the friendship continued throughout their lives until Larkin's death in 1985. Amis was an embodiment of everything that Larkin admired. He was sophisticated and talented academically with a great love and knowledge of jazz, and an irreverent, debunking sense of humour. Together they helped to establish a society of like-minded undergraduates at St John's called 'The Seven', and invented a private code of conversing with each other, a sort of scatological and defamiliarising parlance which became the hallmark of their extensive correspondence through succeeding years.

Larkin in interview said that for him novels had seemed 'richer, broader, deeper, more enjoyable than poems' and that he wanted to "'be a novelist" in a way I never wanted to "be a poet"'(*RW* 63). However, his reputation during his Oxford years was based on his poetry and he contributed poems to publications such as *Phoenix*, *Cherwell*, *Arabesque* and *Oxford Poetry 1942–43*, some of them to an extent derivative from his major influence at this time, W. H. Auden, and with signs towards the end of his university career of the influence of W. B. Yeats, usually ascribed to encountering at the Oxford English Club the Welsh poet Vernon Watkins, who admired Yeats intensely. The interest in prose, however, continued. Between 1937 and 1940, while still a schoolboy, Larkin had written works of fiction (all subsequently destroyed) amounting to more than a quarter of a million words. In his final year at Oxford, with examinations looming, he began to conceive a new kind of fiction, involving some collaboration with and input from Kingsley Amis, under the pseudonym, 'Brunette Coleman', a name inspired by Blanche Coleman, a jazz musician and leader of an all-girl band of the time. The three years after he left Oxford in the Summer of 1943 saw in Larkin an astonishing burst of creativity, surprising in a man later renowned for the comparative sparseness of his poetic output. In these years he managed to produce two novels, *Jill* (completed 1944) and *A Girl In Winter* (completed 1945),[1] as well as a first collection of poetry, *The North Ship* (published 1945). As he himself said of this period, 'As far as my writing was concerned, leaving Oxford was like taking a cork out of a bottle. Writing flooded out of me'.[2] The 'Brunette Coleman' work, written concurrently but not collected until 2002, is of particular interest in any assessment of Larkin's psychology and personality, namely for the light it throws on his youthful sexual confusions as well as on aspects of his involvement with the pornographic subculture. This was something which would scandalise some people in the critical establishment later in his life.

The two substantial 'Brunette' works written in the girls' school story idiom, *Trouble at Willow Gables* and *Michaelmas Term at St Bride's* are mildly erotic and deliberately titillating with their share of the usual paraphernalia of schoolgirl crushes, 'athleticism',

---

1   Published 1946 and 1947 respectively.
2   Quoted in Motion, p.103.

cross-dressing and corporal punishment. But they also go beyond extremely accomplished pastiche to reveal a feminine disposition in Larkin. There is evidence of this in the poetry, too, and a period of bi-sexuality seems to have characterised his personal life at this time.[1] 'Brunette Coleman' also writes a poem sequence entitled *Sugar and Spice*, a collection of seven poems, two of which derive from Larkin's reading in the poetry of Villon and Baudelaire, while other European influences in the 'Brunette' *oeuvre* are an early indication of Larkin's much wider acquaintance with European art and literature than his later dismissive remarks about it would lead readers to believe. The 'Brunette Coleman' fiction is of central interest, too, in that it appears in Larkin's first published novel, *Jill*. Here the lower middle-class protagonist, John Kemp (a fictionalised version of the undergraduate Larkin himself), invents a 'phantom' sister at a boarding school, 'Willow Gables', to whom he writes letters and whose 'diary' he invents in order to create an impressive fiction around himself for the benefit of Christopher Warner, the public schoolboy he secretly admires and with whom he shares rooms. 'Brunette Coleman', the writer, survives until 1946 where 'she' collaborates with Kingsley Amis to produce a work on a lesbian theme, *I Would Do Anything For You*, and then is heard from no more.

By the age of twenty five, therefore, Larkin had published, impressively, two novels and a collection of poems, and had written as much again in unpublished form. The novel with which he followed up *Jill*, *A Girl In Winter*, is written significantly from the female point of view and, like *Jill*, is a work of social realism, focussing, as so much of his poetry would do, on loneliness, unfulfilment and the essential solitude of the individual. Both novels are impressive: *A Girl In Winter* approximates, at its best, to the fiction of James Joyce in stories such as 'The Dead'.[2] Larkin's ambition to be a writer of novels continued and it is clear that he was frustrated by his inability to bring a third one into being. There is evidence that he probably still had hopes of this happening as late as 1954, but his future lay with poetry

1   See Booth, James, ed., Introduction to *Philip Larkin: Trouble at Willow Gables and Other Fictions*, (London: Faber, 2002), *SL*, 40, 46, 68 and 'I see a girl dragged by the wrists', *CP* 278.

2   See *Dubliners* (1914).

and his abandonment of fiction seems to have been coterminous with the enormous success of Kingsley Amis's *Lucky Jim*, published in that year, on which he had substantially collaborated with Amis. The shape of Larkin's undergraduate life is briefly and entertainingly outlined in the 'Introduction' which he wrote for the republication of *Jill* in 1964. It gives sketches of his immediate circle of friends, all male, with the one exception of Diana Gollancz, daughter of the publisher Victor Gollancz, to whom he was obviously attracted but who, like so many of his female acquaintances, represented for him the kind of difficulties that always seemed to beset his relationships with the opposite sex.

1.3 Early career

Larkin graduated from Oxford in 1943 with a First class degree in English and spent the rest of the year living at Warwick with his parents while applying to the Civil Service for various posts. When these failed to materialise he applied for a job as a librarian in the small town of Wellington in Shropshire. Although librarianship was at this time something he casually entered into, his natural aptitude and professionalism transformed the library in Wellington and put him on a course for a career which would take him to libraries at the University of Leicester (1946), Queen's University, Belfast (1950), and finally to be Librarian at the University of Hull in 1955. There he remained for the rest of his life. Library work was congenial to Larkin's temperament. 'Librarianship suits me', he said in interview, 'I love the feel of libraries—and it has just the right blend of academic interest and administration that seems to match my particular talents' (*RW* 51). While beset by the necessities of employment and the familiar pressures which emerge at the threshold of a career, Larkin was busily writing. Living at home in the second half of 1943 he continued to work at the novel, *Jill*, which he had begun at Oxford, completing it at Warwick in the Spring of 1944 and with the help of his friend, Bruce Montgomery, submitting it initially and unsuccessfully to various high profile publishers such as Faber and Gollancz. Eventually it was accepted by the small Fortune Press in the late

Summer of 1944 and published in October 1946. In 1944 the Fortune Press was also compiling an anthology edited by a Merton College undergraduate, William Bell, called *Poetry from Oxford in Wartime,* to which Larkin was invited to submit some of his poems. When it was published it contained ten poems by Larkin written between 1943 and 1944. Before its publication, however, the proprietor of the Press, J. A. Caton, also invited some of the anthology's contributors to submit work for individual consideration. Larkin duly complied and it was the Fortune Press which went on to publish his first collection of poems, *The North Ship* in July 1945.

The North Ship contained thirty one poems, of which ten were transposed from *Poetry from Oxford in Wartime*. When the collection was reissued by Faber in 1966 Larkin added, 'As a coda', a poem, 'Waiting for breakfast'.[1] This had originally been included in what was to be his own privately published collection *XX Poems* (1951) and Larkin's brief 'Introduction' to the reissue refers to it as evidence of the cessation of Yeats's influence which had been very prominent in *The North Ship*. He describes in the 'Introduction' how its 'disappearance' had coincided with his emerging interest in the poetry of Thomas Hardy. Since Anthony Thwaite's edition of Larkin's *Collected Poems* in 1988, much critical attention has been devoted to the poetry of the Oxford years, to *The North Ship* itself, as well as to Larkin's unpublished typescript of twenty five poems *In the Grip of Light* (1947), to try to detect the significance for his mature style of, and the points of transition between, the Yeatsian 'Celtic fever', as Larkin himself decsribes it,[2] and the realism of Hardy and the poets of the thirties. Larkin's own assessment of his poems in *The North Ship*, looking back on them from a distance of thirty years, is that they were 'complete rubbish' (*SL* 374), but recent critics such as Stephen Cooper have seen them as reflecting the social and political realities of their time, taking their cue from writers such as Auden and MacNeice in *Letters from Iceland* (1937) to examine social, moral and gender issues. The poems, according to Cooper, go beyond traditional beliefs 'in seeking alternative principles for human conduct

---

1   *CP* 20.
2   'Introduction' to *The North Ship*, 1966.

that are based on intuition and receptivity to nature'.[1]

In 1946 Larkin left Wellington to take up his new job of Assistant Librarian at the University College of Leicester. He had finished his second novel, *A Girl In Winter*, in the Summer of the previous year and at Leicester he met a university lecturer in English, Monica Jones, with whom he was to form a lifelong, though not a marital, relationship. Monica was Larkin's second serious attachment. His first had been Ruth Bowman, in 1944 a sixteen year old, whom he had met at Wellington library and befriended in the course of their encounters as she borrowed books. This relationship developed to the point of engagement in 1948, although Larkin's announcement of it in a letter to his friend, Jim Sutton, carries his typical note of detachment, suggesting that behind it lay an unwillingness to commit. 'To tell you the truth', he writes, 'I have done something rather odd myself—got engaged to Ruth' (*SL* 147). The engagement would be broken off in 1950 and its story has some significance in the immediate context of Larkin's indeterminacy about whether, during this period of his life, to pursue his career as a writer primarily of poetry or of fiction. 'A very crude difference between novels and poetry', Larkin believed, 'is that novels are about other people and poetry is about yourself'.[2] The problematic conflict between chosen solitude (often described by society as selfishness) and sociability was one of his lifelong preoccupations. Although by no means unsociable, and enjoying his wide circle of friends and associates, Larkin early on expressed in a letter to Sutton his characteristic reserve and the necessity, for him, to prioritise an unimpeded creativity. Here Ruth Bowman appears to be the first of such 'threats' to it.

> I find that once I "give in" to another person, as I have given in not altogether voluntarily, but almost completely, to Ruth, there is a slackening and dulling of the peculiar artistic fibres that makes it impossible to achieve that mental "clenching" that crystallises a pattern and keeps it still while you draw it. (*SL* 116)

---

1   Cooper, Stephen, *Philip Larkin: Subversive Writer* (Brighton: Sussex Academic Press, 2004), 106.

2   Quoted in Motion, Andrew, *Philip Larkin*, (London: Methuen, 1982) p.39.

In 1973 Larkin said that he thought the successful novelist must be interested in other people and he didn't think he was.[1] Certainly, although his inclinations were definitely in the direction of romantic attachments with women, and at later stages in his life he was 'versatile' enough to be able to sustain simultaneous relationships with several, his letters are riddled with remarks on how they compromise his 'priceless liberty' (*SL* 165) and how, as he says to Sutton, he finds it 'easier to abstain from women than sustain the trouble of them & the creakings of my own monastic personality' (*SL* 152). Later, poems such as 'Self's the Man'[2] and 'Vers de Société [3] would dramatise situations in which marriage is seen as the only acceptable alternative to 'selfishness'. An early poem, 'Best Society' (c.1951) concludes with a definite rejection of such a notion. Its speaker retreats to the solitude of his room where his real self and personality can find expression and where, like a sea anemone or snail, 'there cautiously / Unfolds, emerges, what I am.[4]

Larkin's second novel, *A Girl In Winter*, was published by Faber in the February of 1947, and later that same year he compiled a collection of poems, all written after the completion of that novel (1945), and entitled *In the Grip of Light*. Although Faber had recently published *A Girl In Winter* and received Larkin's typescript, they were among several publishers who rejected it. Stephen Regan sees in the title of the collection a tension between 'the constriction of life's possibilities' and a 'sense of affirmation and exaltation'[5] and Stephen Cooper finds that common to nearly all of the poems is 'the theme of entrapment and the quest for new directions and meanings'.[6] These remarks seem to represent and be fairly consistent with Larkin's state of mind

---

1   'Raymond Gardner interviews Dr.Larkin about his Approach to Life and Poetry', *The Guardian* Mar.31, 1973, 12, quoted in Tolley, A.T., *My Proper Ground: A Study of the Work of Philip Larkin and its Development* (Edinburgh: Edinburgh University Press, 1991), p.29.

2   *CP* 117.

3   *CP* 181.

4   *CP* 56.

5   Regan, Stephen, 'In the Grip of Light: Philip Larkin's Poetry of the 1940s', in Booth, James, ed., *New Larkins for Old* (Basingstoke: Palgrave Macmillan, 2000), p.123.

6   Cooper, Stephen, *Philip Larkin: Subversive Writer* (Brighton: Sussex Academic Press, 2004), p.110.

through the mid to late 1940s. His father, Sydney, had died in 1948 and the obligation of caring for his widowed mother, with whom he now shared house, was an additional pressure divided between that, his commitment to his job at Leicester and his engagement to Ruth Bowman. In September 1950 he left Leicester to take up a new post as Sub-Librarian at Queen's University, Belfast and this, to an extent, released him from the restrictions of family and other pressures heralding a much more liberated and creative period, one which would turn out to be among the happiest in his life.

Following perhaps the precedent of Wordsworth in circulating copies of the 1798 *Lyrical Ballads* to important prospective purchasers, in 1951 Larkin despatched copies of a privately published collection, *XX Poems,* to prominent literary figures. Given the significance his poetry would assume just a few years later, *XX Poems* has to be one of the most important neglected publications of the decade. It received practically no acknowledgment, probably because, as Larkin's bibliographer, B. C. Bloomfield, points out, he had put insufficient stamps on the envelopes when the postage rates had just been raised.[1] *XX Poems* contained thirteen poems which might be said to represent Larkin's mature style and which are later included in *The Less Deceived* (1955), and two of them appeared in 1954 in one of the Oxford-based *Fantasy Poets* series of pamphlets (1951–57).[2] *XX Poems* attracted only one critical review which came from the poet and academic D. J. Enright in *The Month*.[3] Larkin would later appear in Enright's anthology, *Poets of the 1950s* (1955) which, together with Robert Conquest's *New Lines: An Anthology* (1956) and G. S. Fraser's *Poetry Now: An Anthology* (1956), reflects a spectrum of poetic talent which came to be known in its time as 'The Movement'. This was a term first used by J. D. Scott, the literary editor of *The Spectator*, in an anonymous leading article in the magazine for 1 October 1954. Here Scott assessed the nature of contemporary poetry as he saw it,

---

1   Bloomfield, B.C., *Philip Larkin: A Bibliography 1933–1994* (London: The British Library, 2002), p. 17.
2   Bloomfield, p.18.
3   *The Month*, n.s. VI (November 1951), p.309.

bored by the despair of the Forties, not much interested in suffering, and extremely impatient of poetic sensibility, especially poetic sensibility about 'the writer and society'...The Movement, as well as being anti-phoney, is anti-wet; sceptical, robust, ironic[...].

Although usually a term taken to describe the poetry of writers such as John Holloway, Donald Davie, Elizabeth Jennings, Thom Gunn, D. J. Enright, Kingsley Amis and Larkin himself, it was broad enough to include writers of fiction like Alan Sillitoe and Larkin's Oxford contemporary, John Wain, as well as so-called 'Angry Young Men' dramatists, among them Arnold Wesker and John Osborne. There are many more names which might be included,[1] but so far as poetry is concerned the general principles adhered to by 'Movement' poetry were described by Robert Conquest in his 'Introduction' to *New Lines*:

If one had briefly to distinguish this poetry of the fifties from its predecessors, I believe the most important general point would be that it submits to no great system of theoretical constructs nor agglomerations of unconscious commands. It is free from both mystical and logical compulsion and—like modern philosophy —is empirical in its attitude to all that comes.

According to Graham Holderness empiricism is 'the basing of thought and action on observation and experiment, rather than theory or idea'[2] and certainly there is a critical consensus that Larkin's poetry does, broadly speaking, reflect such a judgement. The 'technical side' of contemporary poetry, Conquest goes on to remark, involves 'a refusal to abandon a rational structure and comprehensible language, even when the verse is most highly charged with sensual and emotional intent'. Again it is not difficult to see how Larkin might sit with this assessment, although 'The Movement' itself is a very complex pattern of strands and the question as to whether or not Larkin might

---

1   For an important discussion of the period see: Morrison, Blake, *The Movement: English Poetry and Fiction of the 1950s* (London: Methuen, 1980).

2   Holderness, Graham, 'Philip Larkin: the Limits of Experience' in Cookson, Linda and Loughrey, Bryan eds., *Critical Essays on Philip Larkin: The Poems* (London: Longman, 1989), p.112.

be described as a 'Movement' poet, or indeed if there ever was such a thing as 'The Movement' at all, has always been to an extent a debate within Larkin studies. Larkin himself, in a letter to Conquest, and commenting on the *New Lines* Introduction, is careful to place the pronouns 'we' and 'our' in inverted commas when he refers to 'Movement' poetry, though in essence he agrees about such things as 'plain language, absence of posturings, sense of proportion, humour, abandonment of the dithyrambic ideal'. He goes on in the letter to add that poetry is waiting for 'a fuller and more sensitive response to life as it appears from day to day' (*SL* 242).

On the other hand, in 'A Conversation with Ian Hamilton' (1964), Larkin disavowed any sense of belonging to a 'Movement' as such. 'Bob Conquest's *New Lines* in 1956', he says, 'put us all between the same covers. But it certainly never occurred to me that I had anything in common with Thom Gunn, or Donald Davie, for instance, or they with each other' (*FR* 20). This is also in line with what he had written in 1958 in response to an American scholar who was working on 'The Movement'. 'I expect most writers you have approached will vehemently deny any but the slenderest connection with the Movement, and I am no exception'. He goes on to mention among a list of its 'members' those he has never met, acknowledging only intermittent contact with Donald Davie and John Wain and, of course, his close association with Kingsley Amis with whom, he says, he has few artistic aims in common, except for sharing with him the humour that produced the likes of *Lucky Jim* and which he points out is dedicated to him (*SL* 285).

1.4 Hull and fame

Six of Larkin's poems in Robert Conquest's *New Lines* anthology appear in his first major publication, *The Less Deceived,* and Larkin, whose friendship with Conquest developed at this time, had told him of his connection with the small publishing concern of a husband and wife team, George and Jean Hartley, which was run from their terrace house in a suburb of Hull. Along with imprints such as The Fantasy Press, Conquest mentions, in his Introduction to *New Lines*, the Hartleys' 'new Marvell Press' as one example of the small businesses running off limited editions to which many of the poets in his book owed their first publication. Although Larkin at this time was reasonably well established as a published writer, he had submitted poems to the Hartleys' new magazine, *Listen*, which had been so admired by them that they offered to publish a collection of his work. The appearance of *The Less Deceived* with the Marvell Press in 1955 coincided with Larkin's taking up his new appointment as Librarian at the University of Hull, and these years of his early fame and connection with the Hartleys are interestingly, often amusingly, described by Jean Hartley in her book, *Philip Larkin, The Marvell Press and Me*.[1] The rest of Larkin's life would be spent in Hull, a city, he said, which 'neither impresses nor insists' (*FR* 136). He liked it because of its distance from the metropolis and its lonely surrounding landscapes, but given, he said, that the basic requirements of his life were satisfied ('peace, quiet, warmth') he more or less didn't notice where he lived (*RW* 54).

The five years Larkin had spent in Belfast had been a productive time for him and *The Less Deceived* represents the fruition of this period of creativity. Socially, too, Larkin had established and enjoyed good friendships with members of the academic community at Queen's University. His association with women friends also continued, and while Monica Jones was a constant in his life (the woman to whom he dedicated *The Less Deceived*), he added to his 'collection' of friendships Winifred Arnott, a colleague in the library who was already engaged to be married, the married Judy Egerton, a future curator in the Tate Gallery and, more seriously, Patsy Strang, the wife of a philosophy lecturer, Colin Strang, with whom she enjoyed something of an open marriage. Larkin pursued an affair with Patsy who in 1952 conceived his child but suffered a miscarriage.

Larkin had originally given his poem 'Deceptions'[2] the title he now transferred to the collection as a whole. It derives from Ophelia's response to Hamlet who, when he tells her that he'd never loved her,

---

1   Hartley, Jean, *Philip Larkin, The Marvell Press and Me* (Manchester: Carcanet, 1989).
2   *CP* 32.

says 'I was the more deceiv'd'.[1] 'Deceptions', which would later attract unfavourable attention within feminist critical circles in particular, is based on an episode in Henry Mayhew's *London Labour and the London Poor* (1851–52) in which a young girl gives an account of her seduction and rape. The poem's 'message', that the girl was in fact 'less deceived' than her seducer, is the bleakest statement among the twenty nine poems of the collection which more or less conclude that it is wiser to be less deceived about life than to imagine, in the words of the poem 'Next, Please', that 'all we are owed / For waiting so devoutly and so long' will eventually be granted to us. *The Less Deceived*, as is also true of the two later collections, *The Whitsun Weddings* (1964) and *High Windows* (1974), contains at least one poem which can claim to be of major significance. Here it is 'Church Going' of which, Richard Bradford remarks, 'One is aware of that token of excellence, the contrast between the easy, elegant passage of the words and the immense difficulty of making this effect possible'.[2] Speaking of 'Church Going' in a BBC television poetry forum, Stephen Spender singled out Larkin in particular who, he said, 'is my idea of the perfect poet'. Spender thought that Larkin's strength on the whole was in 'progression'. His poems 'begin...travel to an end, and then they *do* end' with, in the case of 'Church Going', he remarks, 'almost sublime lines'.[3] The appearance of 'Church Going' in *The Spectator*,[4] which had mislaid the poem since Larkin had submitted it sixteen months previously, was more or less contemporary with the publication of *The Less Deceived*. On the strength of this poem, Faber's Charles Monteith wrote to Larkin offering to publish any collection of work that he might have. However, the offer was too late as Larkin was already committed to the Marvell Press. The signs of his arrival on the threshold of fame, though, were evident in the critical reception given to *The Less Deceived* after its publication in October, 1955. By the end of the following year it had gone into its third 1500 copy impression, by which time Larkin was already

---

1   *Hamlet*, 3.1.119.
2   Bradford, Richard, *First Boredom, Then Fear: The Life of Philip Larkin* (London: Peter Owen, 2005), p.126.
3   *Poets on Poetry: Eliot and After* (BBCTV, 1988).
4   *The Spectator*, 18 November 1955.

achieving a public profile. In 1956 he made a BBC Third Programme broadcast as part of a series entitled, *New Poetry*,[1] and began regular reviewing for *The Guardian* newspaper.

In October 1956, after having lived in several unsuitable forms of accommodation, Larkin moved into an upper storey flat in a university-owned property at 32 Pearson Park within a residential suburb of Hull. This was to be his home for the next eighteen years, the core period of his professional life as Librarian where he established and oversaw the two-stage construction of what would become the university's prestigious Brynmor-Jones Library. Larkin's career as a librarian was enormously successful. He had first class administrative skills, was popular with his staff, and during the course of his tenure he revealed additional talents in his quick grasp of architectural planning and design issues as the library expanded. After the success of *The Less Deceived*, and from this point onwards in his literary career, Larkin worked very deliberately and very slowly, producing between 1956 and 1960 fewer than three poems a year on average. His full-time preoccupation with his job probably goes a long way to accounting for this and his daily routine, he said, became a dividing of his time between cooking, eating, washing-up, phone calls, 'hack writing, drink and television' (*RW* 57). This emphasis on an unremarkable pattern of existence, the uneventful ordinariness of his life, tends with Larkin to be part of a characteristic laying of false trails. On the other hand, routine seems to have had for him a self-protecting purpose which he made clear in interview: 'I suppose everyone tries to ignore the passing of time: some people by doing a lot, being in California one year and Japan the next; or there's my way—making every day and every year exactly the same' (*RW* 57–58).

From 1960, Larkin began to establish a relationship with a young colleague in his library, Maeve Brennan, who, as the years went on, became his alternative 'option' for the long-standing connection with Monica Jones. The relationship with Maeve continued until 1978, in the course of which Larkin also began an affair with his secretary of sixteen years, Betty Mackereth. Although the popular public perception of him was always that of the sequestered librarian and,

---

1   BBC Third Programme, 13 April 1956.

in Andrew Motion's term, the 'Parnassian Ron Glum'[1], Larkin was
in fact capable of an amazing measure of sexual intrigue and con-
cealment in his private life. He shows an unusual skill for manipu-
lation and a dexterity at being involved with several people at the
same time, playing them off one against the other and coping with the
attendant emotional complexities. Aspects of his temperament which
reveal the complicated and multi-faceted individual he really was are
brought out interestingly in *The Philip Larkin I Knew*, an account by
Maeve Brennan of her intimate knowledge of him and published in
2002.[2]

If *The Less Deceived* had brought Larkin to the attention of the
public as, in the words of the anonymous reviewer in the *Times
Literary Supplement*, 'a poet of quite exceptional importance',[3] his
next collection of 1964, *The Whitsun Weddings*, compounded that
status. By now Larkin had abandoned George Hartley's Marvell
Press and it was Faber which subsequently became his publisher.
Like its predecessor, *The Whitsun Weddings* was a slim volume of
verse containing in total only three more poems, but it consolidates
what many feel to be the true Larkin 'voice', a voice less reminis-
cent of the earlier Yeatsian and Symbolist influences still traceable
in *The Less Deceived*. Its immediate success resulted in Larkin being
awarded the Queen's Gold Medal for Poetry in 1965 and led to his
appearance as the subject of a television programme for the BBC's
Monitor series in which he was filmed on his home ground in Hull,
at work in the library and in his flat at Pearson Park, with much of
the broadcast showing him in conversation with his admired John
Betjeman. Larkin had always regarded Betjeman as a central figure
in twentieth-century English verse, writing of him as someone 'who
restored direct intelligible communication to poetry' (*RW* 217), while
at the same time by extolling Betjeman's virtues, as Andrew Motion
writes, helping 'to create the taste by which he wished his own work

---

1   'Ron Glum' was a lugubrious comic character in the BBC Radio series *Take It
    From Here* in the1950s.
2   Brennan, Maeve, *The Philip Larkin I Knew* (Manchester: Manchester University
    Press, 2002).
3   The reviewer was Michael Hamburger. See Hamburger, Michael, *Philip Larkin*
    (London: Enitharmon Press, 2002).

to be judged'.[1]

By this time Larkin had become so highly regarded that he was approached in 1966 by Oxford University Press as a possible editor for its proposed *Oxford Book of Twentieth Century English Verse*. The previous editor had been W. B. Yeats in *The Oxford Book of Modern Verse* in 1936, so Larkin was especially gratified to have been nominated and allowed his name to go forward. He was accepted and his subsequent editorship involved him in five years of preparation. It included two terms as Visiting Fellow at All Souls College, Oxford in 1970–71 where he worked on the Bodleian Library's collections, and the anthology appeared in March 1973 to a mixed and sometimes hostile reception. Larkin describes in his brief Introduction to the book his principal aims in compiling it. First of all, to include poems 'judged either by the age or by myself to be worthy of inclusion', secondly, 'poems judged by me to be worthy of inclusion without reference to their authors', and thirdly, 'poems judged by me to carry with them something of the century in which they were written'.

In his preliminary letter to Dan Davin of the Oxford University Press Larkin had stated that his guiding principle, in general, 'would be to produce a collection of pieces that had delighted me, and so might be expected to delight others'(*SL* 380). This emphasis on the importance of 'delight' in poetry goes back at least as far as Sir Philip Sidney who, in his *An Apology for Poetry* (1581), had stressed that, as well as to teach, the purpose of poetry should be to move and to delight. In a piece written in 1957, 'The Pleasure Principle', Larkin said that 'at bottom poetry, like all art, is inextricably bound up with giving pleasure, and if a poet loses his pleasure-seeking audience he has lost the only audience worth having'(*RW* 81–82). One of the arts which in Larkin's opinion had lost, or was in danger of losing, its pleasure-seeking audience was jazz music. From 1961 until 1970 he was the regular jazz reviewer for *The Daily Telegraph*, and in 1970 Faber published a book of these writings entitled, *All What Jazz*. Although he claimed no more than amateur status for himself, Larkin was in fact immensely knowledgeable about this subject and the Introduction, in particular, which he wrote for the Faber collec-

---

1   Motion, p. 292.

tion has since become notorious for the attack it includes, not only on modern jazz, but also on Modernism in general (represented here by Larkin's selecting Charlie Parker, Pound and Picasso) for having exploited technique in contradiction, he writes, 'of human life as we know it'. Modernism, he goes on, 'helps us neither to enjoy nor endure. It will divert us as long as we are prepared to be mystified or outraged, but maintains its hold only by being more mystifying and more outrageous: it has no lasting power'.[1] In a footnote to the revised edition of 1985, Larkin was even less compromising when he added that he was using 'these pleasantly alliterative names [Parker, Pound, Picasso] to represent not only their rightful owners but every prac-titioner who might be said to have succeeded them'. Critical exami-nation of Larkin's work, however, has revealed his indebtedness to Modernism, and statements such as these must always be carefully placed within a broader historical and contextual frame of reference.

Exactly a decade after the publication of *The Whitsun Weddings* Larkin's final collection, *High Windows*, appeared in 1974. Once again, a slim volume of only twenty four poems, it contained this time a wider range of subject materials, with some poems such as 'This be the Verse' and 'Annus Mirabilis' written in a demotic reg-ister, and others like 'Solar' and 'The Explosion' owing more to Symbolist influences. Two poems in particular, 'The Old Fools' and 'The Building' represented, as in previous collections, larger reflec-tions on, and characteristic preoccupations with, illness, age and death. *High Windows* was immediately successful, selling over twenty thousand copies within twelve months of publication. Yet from this point onwards there would be no further collections. Between 1974 and his death in 1985 Larkin published only a handful of poems, most of them very brief, with the exception of one last major work, 'Aubade'. This was written three months before the publication of *High Windows* and appeared just before Christmas 1977 in the *Times Literary Supplement*.[2]

As his creative capacities seemed to dwindle as he aged, Larkin's

---

1   Larkin, Philip, *All What Jazz: A Record Diary* (London: Faber, 1970) Introduction.
2   *Times Literary Supplement*, 23 December 1977.

personal life, always to a degree complicated, became less and less satisfactory to him. In 1974 he had had to vacate his university-owned flat and for the first time purchase a house. He chose a modern and unremarkable detached property at 105 Newlands Park in Hull. He still worked efficiently in his post as Librarian, was made the recipient of numerous awards and honorary degrees, was offered and rejected the Poet Laureateship on the death of John Betjeman, but seemed on evidence to become increasingly reactionary and intolerant. His letters reveal a catalogue of dislikes, no longer simply those for which he could sometimes express an amusing distaste: poet contemporaries, academics, even children and Christmas, to be sure, but also more troublesome issues for him, like modern England's laziness and the proliferation of the work-shy, student protests, the power of the Trades Unions and mass immigration. When his forthright, often racist and misogynistic, remarks surfaced after his death in Anthony Thwaite's *Selected Letters* and Andrew Motion's official biography in the early 1990s, they were inevitably, for many, a shock, and damaging to his reputation. Consequently, Larkin's work was often marginalised or even excluded from programmes and syllabuses, especially in 'liberal' academic communities, and it is only gradually beginning to recover from this. These issues will be returned to in the final section.

In the early 1980s Larkin's health began to deteriorate. From 1983 his long-term association with Monica Jones became a marriage in all but name when, after suffering an illness, she moved in permanently with him at Newlands Park. Throughout his life Larkin had smoked, and had become an increasingly heavy drinker. Various illnesses in his past had always proved to be false alarms, but in 1985 he was diagnosed with cancer of the oesophagus from which he died on 2 December of that year. He was buried at Cottingham on 9 December. His gravestone is marked simply 'Philip Larkin: Writer', and in February of the following year a memorial service was held for him at Westminster Abbey.

Part 2: Artistic strategies

2.1 The Profession of poetry

From his early schooldays Larkin was devoted to the craft of poetry. James Booth remarks on how writing was almost a physical pleasure for him as he sewed his juvenile poems into little booklets, using different colours of ink, art paper and patternings of letters. This 'absorbed world of rapt creation',[1] as Booth describes it, is evident in the painstaking processes of poetical composition to be found in his work book revisions, and continued throughout his life.[2] It calls particularly to mind a poet like William Blake whose meticulously 'crafted' output reflects a similar single-minded purpose in the vocation Larkin pursued. 'You see', Larkin (aged 22) writes in a letter to Norman Iles, 'my trouble is that I simply can't understand anybody doing anything but write, paint, compose music' (*SL* 88). This total dedication to his art is comparable to what David Dubal recalls of the legendary pianist, Vladimir Horowitz:

> Horowitz's involvement with the piano was so absolute that he actually wondered what people who were not pianists did with their time. With Flaubert, he could ask, 'Why is he in the world? And what is he doing here, poor wretch? I cannot imagine how people unconcerned with art can spend their time; how they live is a mystery to me'.[3]

Thus Larkin, in his letter to Iles, wonders what he should do if, after a day's work or a 'ghastly' half hour he couldn't 'start work

---

1 Booth, James, *Philip Larkin: The Poet's Plight* (Basingstoke: Palgrave Macmillan, 2005), p.5
2 See Tolley, A.T., *Larkin at Work: A Study of Larkin's Mode of Composition as seen in his Workbooks* (Hull: Hull University Press, 1997).
3 Dubal, David, *Evenings with Horowitz: A Personal Portrait* (London: Robson Books, 1992), p.xx.

again' by writing about the experiences he had assimilated—'And all the people who don't think like this,' he wonders, 'what do they do?' After such speculation, however, he draws back, adding 'Somehow this is all rather pompous, & not quite what I meant. I wonder if you get the hang of it'. To get the hang of it is to understand simply that Larkin indulges no false modesty. Although he is speaking slightly facetiously when he remarks of his first meeting with Kingsley Amis, 'For the first time I felt myself in the presence of a talent greater than my own' (*RW* 20), there is an element of truth in it also. He had a very solid sense of his own worth, recalling Keats's strictures on his contemporaries—Wordsworth for example, one of the 'large self-worshippers,' and Byron, a hectorer in 'proud bad verse'—'Tho' I breathe death with them it will be life / To see them sprawl before me into graves'.[1] Larkin has a similarly refreshing irreverence for his fellow practitioners—'Who cares about asses like Blake or bores like Byron!' (*SL* 294). Yeats is a 'posturing old ass' (*SL* 315). Ted Hughes, whose poetry leaves him 'stern curled' (*SL* 677) is 'no good at all' (*SL* 396) and he looks forward to reviews of the '*Penguin* [Book] of Contemp verse'[2] to see 'who they can possibly pretend is worth a finch's fart' (*SL* 680). Just as Keats, however, would have been the first to profess his real admiration for Wordsworth and appreciate the talent of Byron, Larkin himself owed an enormous debt to predecessors such as Yeats, posturing old ass though he may have described him. His concern is only to establish with confidence the credentials he possessed which could enable him to say with Keats, 'I think I shall be among the English poets after my death'.

Larkin was given to throw-away remarks on what he took most seriously. So writing poems was a 'cheap way of enjoying oneself' (*SL* 349), a sort of 'verbal photography' (*FR* 87). His poem 'Dublinesque' was the product of a dream, 'I just woke up and described it',[3] he says, or for example 'The Whitsun Weddings' 'only needed writing down. Anybody could have done it' (*FR* 57). These kinds of comment reflect Larkin's concern to re-establish poetry as 'an affair of

---

1   *The Fall of Hyperion*, ll.207-10.
2   Morrison, Blake and Motion, Andrew., *The Penguin Book of Contemporary British Poetry* (Harmondsworth: Penguin, 1982).
3   Quoted in Motion, p. 395.

sanity, of seeing things as they are' (*RW* 197). He said in an essay on John Betjeman that in the twentieth-century English poetry had gone off 'on a loop-line that took it away from the general reader' (*RW* 216). He remarks in aspects of Betjeman's poetry, for example, precisely those elements which could be said to make up the characteristics of his own poems, 'a defiant advocacy of the little, the obscure, the disregarded' along with 'an outstanding gift for phrasing, not of the smart epigrammatic sort, but that which conjures a picture to fix whatever it is in the hearer's mind for ever' (*RW* 206). Similarly on the novels of Barbara Pym, which he so admired, Larkin's observations throw light on the nature of the poetry he himself writes. He admires their treatment of 'the underlying loneliness of life, the sense of *vulnerant omnes* [...] the absence of self-pity, the scrupulousness of one's relations with others, the small blameless comforts' (*RW* 243–44). These seemingly low-key aspirations for literature have led some critics into an assessment of Larkin's work with its deliberately understated aims as narrow and provincial. Charles Tomlinson, as one example, talks of Larkin's 'wry and sometimes tenderly nursed sense of defeat';[1] Donald Davie, another, of his 'poetry of lowered sights and patiently diminished expectations';[2] while, in his Introduction to *The New Poetry* in 1962, A.Alvarez saw Larkin as a representative of what he calls, 'the disease so often found in English culture; gentility'.[3] Yet Larkin's promotion of Betjeman, out of kilter in its time with high criticism's opinion of him as little more than a simplistic versifier, while acknowledging his 'popularity' and his being 'fairly easy to understand', also denies that his poetry is 'simple'. Larkin writes that 'He is complex without being difficult' (*FR* 30), again a statement which could equally be applied to much of his own work whose strategically designed accessibility has led many critics into making erroneous judgements on it.

Larkin had a very carefully thought-out programme for poetry once the first stage, an 'emotional concept', compels the poet, as he says, 'to

1   Tomlinson, Charles, in Ford, Boris ed., *The Pelican Guide to English Literature*, Vol.7, *The Modern Age* (Harmondsworth: Penguin, 3rd. ed., 1973) pp.478–9.
2   Davie, Donald, *Thomas Hardy and British Poetry* (London: Routledge & Kegan Paul, 1973) p.71.
3   Alvarez, A., *The New Poetry* (Harmondsworth: Penguin, 1962), p. 28.

do something about it'. Rather as William Carlos Williams describes a poem as 'a small (or large) machine made of words,' Larkin calls the poem, as product of his 'second stage', 'a verbal device' whose function is to reproduce the emotional concept in anyone who reads it, 'anywhere, at any time'. The 'third stage' becomes a 'recurrent situation' of people 'setting off the device' and so being able to recreate for themselves 'in different times and places' what the poet felt when he wrote it (*RW* 80). The process is not unlike Wordsworth's description of poetry as 'emotion recollected in tranquillity' and indeed emotion is something upon which Larkin puts considerable emphasis in his remarks on the creation and purpose of his writing: 'To me, now as at any other time, poetry should begin with emotion in the poet and end with the same emotion in the reader' (*FR* 65). Thus, in the context of typically asserting 'I have no ideas about poetry at all', Larkin will go on to describe a carefully constructed pattern of impulses which give rise to his poems: 'For me, a poem is the crossroads of my thoughts, my feelings, my imaginings, my wishes & my verbal sense [...] only when all cross at one point do you get a poem' (*SL* 173). This combination of words, therefore, making up a device to 'set off' similar feelings in other people is underpinned by Larkin's much-repeated concern for the preservation of emotion. As Wordsworth, who speaks of his intention to give substance to what he feels in order to 'enshrine' it 'For future restoration,' [1] Larkin speaks of the poem as 'a kind of preservation by re-creation' (*FR* 106) believing that 'the impulse to preserve lies at the bottom of all art' (*RW* 79).

2.2 Dramatic elements

Stephen Spender referred to Larkin giving expression to things in poetry which were unique to him, and yet which a great many people would respond to. He cites 'Church Going' as a 'supreme example', speaking of his ability to create himself as a person within his own poetry.[2] It is this dramatic element in Larkin which has been noted by many critics as well as being remarked upon by the poet him-

---

1   *The Prelude* (1805), 11, ll. 339–42.
2   *Poets and Poetry: Eliot and After* (BBCTV, 1988)

self—'I think one has to dramatise oneself a little.'[1] Stephen Cooper sees Larkin's use of different personae as his means of allowing him to consider experience through different perspectives, and 'it is this *dialectic*', he says, that 'drives many of the poems.'[2] He writes of his narrative and performative techniques being contained within the discipline of the lyric form, and Larkin early on in his career did indeed experiment to some extent with dramatic literature, producing two verse dramas[3] as well as two pieces in the form of a dialogue or debate.[4] Andrew Swarbrick describes Larkin's poems as 'multivocal', calling them 'performative' in the sense that 'They are the dramatised speech-acts of a speaker who, seeming to participate in, actually manipulates, the drama of his poems.'[5] The poems, as Jenny Joseph points out, are indeed dramatic in the primary sense that things happen in them, but the manipulation, noted by Swarbrick, exists for her in that the action 'does not happen to "characters" who Larkin has created by using different voices to tell the action. It happens to the reader, to us'. It is the way we are 'drawn into the poem' which constitutes its action, she argues, even though 'the "matter" that the language is presenting may be very specifically "about" something else.'[6] In the sense that Larkin wanted his poems to reproduce or 'set off' his own emotions as they were read, it is true in the wider sense that the dramatic construction of his poetry has a design upon its readers. Its performative nature takes many forms. It exists, for example, in the presentation of the persona in 'Vers de Société' who stands 'Holding a glass of washing sherry, canted / Over to catch the drivel of some bitch / Who's read nothing but *Which*.' The lines capture per-

---

1   'Four Conversations', talking to Ian Hamilton, *London Magazine*, Vol. iv, No. 6, November, 1964

2   Cooper, Stephen, *Philip Larkin: Subversive Writer* (Brighton: Sussex Academic Press, 2004), p. 39.

3   *Behind the Façade or 'Points of View'*, EPJ., pp. 317–37 and *Night in the Plague*, EPJ., pp.338–46

4   *Round the Point*, Booth, James, ed., *Trouble at Willow Gables and other fictions* (Faber, London, 2002) 471–82 and *Round Another Point, Trouble at Willow Gables*, pp.485–98

5   Swarbrick, Andrew, 'Larkin's Identities' in Regan, Stephen ed., *Philip Larkin* (Basingstoke: Palgrave Macmillan, 1997) pp. 215–16.

6   Joseph, Jenny, 'Larkin the Poet: The Old Fools' in Hartley, George, ed., *Philip Larkin: 1922–1985: A Tribute* (London: The Marvell Press, 1988) p.120.

fectly the posture of the speaker (Larkin himself suffered from deafness in later years) in danger of spilling his (preferred) drink while struggling to catch despised small-talk amidst the din of a social gathering. Sometimes a single line puts a direct onus of responsibility onto its reader for effect. Thus, the final statement of 'Going, Going', 'I just think it will happen, soon,' creates different interpretative possibilities depending on where specific words are made to carry the emphasis. The persona in 'Dockery and Son' involves us in a developing tale made the more convincing by the way the language mimics dramatically the processes of thought: 'Well, it just shows / How much…How little…Yawning, I suppose / I fell asleep' (18–20). Much is owed here to the interiority of Romantic poetry as where, for example, in 'Tintern Abbey' the validity of Wordsworth's elusive experience is often established by the uncertainty of the phrasing which gives expression to the thought process: 'Once again I see / These hedge-rows, hardly hedgerows, little lines / Of sportive wood'; 'Nor less, I trust'; 'If this / Be but a vain belief, yet, oh! How oft', and so on. Similarly, Larkin's settled lack of conviction is convincingly dramatised in the self-critical, self-consciousness of self-corrected lines such as,

> Dockery, now:
> Only nineteen, he must have taken stock
> Of what he wanted, and been capable
> Of…No, that's not the difference: rather how
>
> Convinced he was he should be added to! (29–33)

or those in 'Vers de Société' where the persona critiques his own argument, 'Too subtle, that. Too decent, too. Oh hell [...]'

Larkin's assessment of the dramatic nature of situations has, in common with Shakespeare, an understanding of the possibility that men are no more than actors and their world a play. In *Hamlet* the trope is particularly prominent where to 'act' in the sense of 'to do' (something Hamlet finds difficult) becomes effectively to act in the sense of 'perform'. *Hamlet*'s recognition that a play is a kind of scheme for the human condition is reflected in many terms which suggest the theatrical quality of the life it depicts ('act', 'perform', 'put on', 'motive', 'cue', 'audience', and so on) as well as its hero's awareness of his own 'part' in the drama ('Or I could make a prologue to my brains, / They had begun the play').[1] Throughout Larkin's poems from *The Less Deceived* to *High Windows* runs a consciousness of life as drama and of the self as having a role within it. 'Wild Oats' begins, 'About twenty years ago / Two girls came in where I worked'. The girls arrive on his particular scene as though making their entrance stage left. Having taken (8) one of them out the speaker later parts from her 'after about five / Rehearsals' (17). In 'Absences' it is as if the inconsequential presence of the speaker on the world's stage could be being observed by an unseen audience from 'lit-up galleries' (8). In 'Places, Loved Ones', having missed in life that *'proper ground'* (3) and 'special one' (5) is 'to act' says Larkin, 'As if what you settled for / Mashed you' (18–20).[2] 'Skin' presents flesh as a form of costume worn as a 'daily dress' but one that cannot, as in the theatre, be changed. The ageing costume is told—'You must learn your lines' (4). In 'Show Saturday' the dismantling of the annual fair commences as horse boxes depart 'Like shifting scenery' (39). Larkin's dramatic sense shares a Shakespearean consciousness that life is no more than the 'two hours' traffic' of the stage[3], the 'baseless fabric'[4] of a vision.

2.3 Forms and techniques

Consideration of Shakespeare in this context is of interest, too, in that the questioning nature of a tragedy such as *Hamlet*, for example, depicting characters seeking answers they can never quite find, reflects on the interrogative nature of many of Larkin's poems. Equally intrinsic to Shakespeare is the depiction of man as an actor playing different parts, so that what he seems to be at any one instant, is not necessarily what he will be at the next. Although he may think he is responsible for the role which he plays, he finds often that it

---

1   *Hamlet*, 5.2.30.
2   My emphasis.
3   *Romeo and Juliet*, Prologue, 12.
4   *The Tempest*, 4.1.151.

has been scripted for him by an unseen playwright. 'Our wills and fates do so contrary run,' says the Player King in *Hamlet,* 'That our devices still are overthrown / Our thoughts are ours, their ends none of our own.' [1] At the end of 'Dockery and Son' the speaker's understanding is presented similarly,

> Life is first boredom, then fear.
> Whether or not we use it, it goes,
> And leaves what something hidden from us chose [...]
> (45–47)

The sense of doubt and uncertainty in life, therefore, implicit in the dramatic mode itself, is central to Larkin's work. His speculations lead to the kind of bafflement we encounter in 'Ignorance'—'Strange to know nothing, never to be sure / Of what is true or right or real, / But forced to qualify *or so I feel.*' Many of the poems begin with a question, 'What are days for?'[2], 'What do they think has happened, the old fools, / To make them like this?' [3] Or they contain questions: 'Where do these / Innate assumptions come from?'[4]; 'Where has it gone, the lifetime?'[5]

Creating a sense of instability and uncertainty is a strategy Larkin adopts and deploys by different means throughout his work. Sometimes it is achieved by the use of the present participle instead of a finite verb, 'Unresting death,'[6] 'Coming up England by a different line,'[7] 'solving that question.'[8] Even a conclusive word, 'stop', is allowed a continued momentum, 'Stopping the diary'.[9] Sometimes the use of a parenthetical phrase—'The headed paper, made for writing home / (If home existed),'[10] can produce the effect, as it does here, of nudging us away from any comforting idea of domesticity and secu-

---

1 *Hamlet*, 3. 2. 211–13.
2 *CP* 67.
3 *CP* 196.
4 *CP* 153.
5 *CP* 195.
6 *CP* 208.
7 *CP* 81.
8 *CP* 67.
9 *CP* 184.
10 *CP* 163.

rity. The complexity of the syntactical construction which concludes 'Mr Bleaney' beginning, 'I know' (15) but concluding, 'I don't know' (28), is typical of the chronic sense of doubt and indeterminacy in Larkin which has the effect of alerting the reader to the unreliability of anything which might even hint at firm conviction—the opening of 'Church Going', for example, 'Once I am sure [...].'

Stephen Cooper has remarked that 'Larkin was obsessed with the coexistence in the psyche of oppositional selves that continually vie for control.'[1] This 'dialectic between the *either* and the *or*' the critic John Osborne points out as a strength in Larkin, a liberating element in the poetry, establishing 'as a principle of freedom that one should not be convicted for lacking conviction.'[2] And it shares, too, with the *Innocence* and *Experience* lyrics of Blake, for example, a dialectical mode of thinking rather than presenting an attitude of mind or fixed philosophical position.

Larkin, as we have seen, was drawn initially to the novel, and it was to be known as a writer of fiction for which he nursed ambitions. Although he had abandoned his schemes in this direction certainly by the mid 1950s, it is clear from many of the poems that in terms of plot, characterisation and setting, the techniques of the novelist are still very much at work. Until the arrival on the English literary scene of the great nineteenth-century novels, stories were much more likely to be written in verse than in prose. Narrative verse dominates the major output of the Romantic poets, for example, and although it survives in some of the work of Victorian poets like Browning, Arnold and Tennyson, the freer, more expansive, opportunities offered by the novel effectively ensured that the future of story-telling would lie with fiction. In the twentieth-century, verse narrative had been more or less marginalised, although it could be found, albeit in briefer form, in poems such as Eliot's 'Prufrock', or in some of the poetry of Thomas Hardy, like his narrative 'Outside the Window', for example. Larkin's poetry keeps this tradition very much alive—'To the Sea', 'Show Saturday', 'Church Going', 'Dockery and Son', 'The Whitsun

---

1   Cooper, Stephen, *Philip Larkin: Subversive Writer* (Brighton: Sussex Academic Press, 2004) p. 148.

2   Osborne, John, *Larkin, Ideology and Critical Violence: A Case of Wrongful Conviction* (Basingstoke: Palgrave Macmillan, 2008) p.105.

Weddings', are just a few prominent instances of where the art of fiction in the creation of a character within the narrative can be realised vividly, in lines often relaying the processes of his or her movements as the story unfolds, for example—'I try the door of where I used to live: / Locked',[1] or 'Hatless, I take off / My cycle-clips in awkward reverence.'[2]

Larkin shows great skill, too, in his effortless ability to write colloquially or conversationally within the strict parameters of rhyme and verse structure. 'Poetry of Departures' allows the sense of three of its eight line stanzas to run on, while at the same time adopting a complicated ABCBADCD rhyme scheme composed of full and half rhymes. The art which conceals art produces the natural speech register of the poem. Similarly, 'No Road' achieves a seamless blend of conversational voice and sustained metaphysical conceit so that, as Alun R. Jones has remarked, it directs attention almost 'away from the poem as a poem towards the feeling for direct speech and intonation, towards almost casual utterance.' The terms of the metaphor employed are precisely described but without, he says, 'calling attention to the metaphor itself.'[3] In these respects Larkin is an exceptional technician, sharing ability with the greatest poets working within traditional forms to produce their own voice.

He himself, however, denied that he had any particular interest in technicalities. 'Form holds little interest for me,' he wrote, 'Content is everything.'[4] On this, James Booth has remarked that in Larkin's work, nevertheless, form and content are so much a part of each other that either Larkin's is a misleading judgement or a proof 'of the truism that form is content.'[5] Larkin's employment of various forms range from the simple 'emblem poem' of the seventeenth-century in the manner of George Herbert's 'Easter Wings' or 'The Altar', for example, in a poem such as 'Wires', to the 'rhetorical majesty,' in

---

1   *CP* 152.

2   *CP* 97.

3   Jones, Alun R., *The Poetry of Philip Larkin: A Note on Transatlantic Culture* in Chambers, Harry, ed., *Phoenix*, 11/12, 1973–74, p.148.

4   Quoted in Timms, David, *Philip Larkin* (Edinburgh: Oliver & Boyd, 1973), p. 62.

5   Booth, James, *Philip Larkin: The Poet's Plight* (Basingstoke: Palgrave Macmillan, 2005), p.14. Larkin's technicalities receive detailed critical attention in Chapter 1.

Clive James's words,[1] of the larger stanza form of eight lines ('Show Saturday', 'Dockery and Son', 'Here'), nine ('Church Going', 'To the Sea', 'The Whitsun Weddings') and more ('The Old Fools'). Form and content skilfully reflect each other in the structure of 'The Whitsun Weddings', where the leisurely nine-line stanza form communicates 'all sense / Of being in a hurry gone' (4–5) and the short dimeter in each creates the pause made by the 'slow and stopping' (11) train as it journeys southwards.

'Nothing so difficult as a beginning / In poetry', writes Byron in *Don Juan*, 'unless perhaps the end'.[2] Larkin is, on Byron's terms, supremely qualified as a poet who can resolve memorably the difficulty of concluding. Gavin Ewart praises this talent in, for example, the last line of 'The Old Fools' and 'Vers de Société,[3] while Christopher Ricks, also, remarks on Larkin's 'effortless accuracy of conclusion'.[4] David Timms thinks that Larkin's endings are memorable, not because they are 'resounding or aphoristic', but because 'they catch the mood of the poem as a whole in a few words.'[5] Larkin's poems have a typical progression, and so carefully has their subject been thought through that their endings seem somehow inevitable. The progression in his poetry can take the form of a change in personal pronoun, 'Once I am sure there's nothing going on', evolving significantly to an inclusive 'wondering, too / When churches fall completely out of use / What *we* shall turn them into'[6] (my emphasis). It can be tonal, in what Stephen Regan identifies as the shift from 'colloquial banter to sombre meditation' in 'Next Please'.[7] Or the progression may consist in what George Hartley sees as Larkin's great strength, his 'working from the particular to the universal'.[8] One such example might be the development in the six-line 'As Bad

1   James, Clive, *At the Pillars of Hercules* (London: Faber, 1979), p. 69
2   *Don Juan*, 4, ll.1–2.
3   *Poetry Review*, 1982, 2
4   Ricks, Christopher, *The Whitsun Weddings* in Chambers, Harry ed., *Phoenix* 11/12, 1973–74, p. 10.
5   Timms, David, *Philip Larkin* (Edinburgh: Oliver & Boyd, 1973), p.107.
6   'Church Going', ll. 1/21–23.
7   Regan, Stephen, *Philip Larkin* (Basingstoke: Macmillan, 1992), p. 90.
8   Hartley, George, 'No Right of Entry: Dry Point' in Hartley, George, ed., *Philip Larkin 1922-1985: A Tribute* (London: The Marvell Press, 1988), p. 136.

as a Mile' from the unremarkable *failure* to get a 'shied' apple core into a basket, to the *failure* brought upon all mankind by Eve's *failure* to resist the tempting apple in the first place. In this poem, the structural development *from* time-present *to* Garden of Eden runs contrariwise to the historical progression *from* Eve *to* speaker. The brief poem 'Days' similarly develops from an almost childlike simplicity in the innocence of its first question, 'What are days for?', to a disturbing realisation of the imponderables presenting themselves at the end of every human life.

2.4 Romantic connections

In a celebrated essay on Larkin, 'The Main of Light' (1988),[1] Seamus Heaney identifies visionary elements in the poetry recalling for him such moments in Shakespeare where, in Sonnet 60, for example, the line, 'Nativity, once in the main of light' removes us from ' a world of discourse' and makes an unpredictable 'strike into the realm of pure being [...].'[2] A similarity in Larkin, and mentioned by Heaney, is the conclusion to 'Here', with its progression on a journey eastwards, through city and countryside, to the seashore where 'ends the land suddenly' (30). The poem's title comes to be incorporated into the final statement, 'Here is unfenced existence: / Facing the sun, untalkative, out of reach' (32), and the apprehension of a 'bluish neutral distance', whose meaning eludes expression ('untalkative'), brings the poem to its visionary conclusion. This poem from *The Whitsun Weddings* anticipates the title poem 'High Windows' from the 1974 collection. Here a crude expression at the start heralds the poem's all too familiar concern with regrets and frustration, but resolves into the transcendent finish,

> And immediately

> Rather than words comes the thought of high
> windows:

---

1   Heaney, Seamus, 'The Main of Light' in Thwaite, Anthony, ed., *Larkin at Sixty* (London: Faber, 1982), pp.131-38.
2   Heaney, p.131.

> The sun-comprehending glass,
> And beyond it, the deep blue air, that shows
> Nothing, and is nowhere, and is endless.

Larkin's use of language to engage with a visionary dimension and communicating an elusiveness in the expression of it, has its counterpart in the effects sometimes magnificently achieved by Wordsworth. Thus, in the course of his revision of 'Elegiac Stanzas suggested by a Picture of Peele Castle in a Storm', Wordsworth altered part of the following lines,

> Ah! THEN, if mine had been the Painter's hand,
> To express what then I saw; and add the gleam,
> The light that never was, on sea or land
> The consecration, and the Poet's dream.'

to:

> and add a gleam
> Of lustre, known to neither sea nor land
> But borrowed from the youthful Poet's dream.

Tellingly, he later restored the lines of the original stanza, obviously recognising their superior expression in conveying a sense that visionary intelligence is intrinsic to the poet and not simply something attached to him as something external from which he can 'borrow'. Larkin's poetry here reveals its affiliation with the poetry of the Romantics, sharing the problems Romantic poetry in particular sometimes encountered with the adequacy of language in the expression of elusive modes of consciousness.

In *The Prelude* Wordsworth makes, he says, no more than 'Breathings for incommunicable powers' for what lies 'in the main [...] far hidden from the reach of words'.[1] In *Childe Harold* Byron wants to 'wreak / [his] thoughts upon expression', but as it is, he writes, 'I live and die unheard, / With a most voiceless thought'.[2] For Shelley a poem is simply an inadequate, if generous, attempt

---

1 Wordsworth: *The Prelude* (1805), 3, 184–85, 188.
2 Byron: *Childe Harold's Pilgrimage*, 3, 906–7, 912–13.

to repeat its original inspiration,[1] and in Blake the spontaneity of the 'Introduction' to *Songs of Innocence* is systematically eroded as the happy 'piping' with which it opens 'degenerates' into repetition and the fixed form of the written word. In *The Marriage of Heaven and Hell* Blake traces 'the method by which knowledge is transmitted from generation to generation', eventually taking 'the forms of books' to be 'arranged in libraries'. The librarian, Larkin, who famously concludes a poem, 'Books are a load of crap'[2] repeatedly queries the efficacy of language—'but why put it into words?'[3] The Platonic 'padlocked cube of light',[4] the 'untalkative', 'unfenced existence' of 'Here' (31–32) and 'Rather than words' the 'thought of high windows'[5] represent that 'longing for some adjacent "pure serene,"' as Heaney puts it,[6] a dimension in which language can somehow be evaded. 'Painting must be a good way of working', wrote Larkin to his artist friend, Jim Sutton, 'no words, no drivelling "probability" or "construction"—only the pure vision' (*SL* 145). Several of his poems are traceable in their ideas to Keats's 'Ode on a Grecian Urn' where the integrity of a work of art, consisting here in the urn's eloquent silence, is felt to be diminished when forced into 'expression' by the poet.

Keats's concept of the 'poetical Character' involves a loss of identity in the poet,[7] noted in Larkin by Andrew Gibson where 'Loss of self', he writes, 'is something he associated with poetry.' He adds that more important still 'he can associate loss or absence of self with exhilaration or vision.'[8] In interview Larkin said, 'One longs for infinity and absence, the beauty of somewhere you're not,'[9] and he was drawn, probably under the influence initially of Vernon Watkins,

1 P. B. Shelley: *A Defence of Poetry*.
2 'A Study of Reading Habits', *CP* 131.
3 'Love Again', *CP* 215, 11.
4 'Dry Point', *CP* 36, 14.
5 'High Windows' *CP* 165, 17.
6 Heaney in Thwaite, ed., *Larkin at Sixty*, p. 131.
7 Keats, Letter to Richard Woodhouse, 27 October, 1818.
8 Gibson, Andrew, 'Larkin and ordinariness', in Cookson, Linda and Loughrey, Bryan, *Critical Essays on Philip Larkin: The Poems* (Harlow: Longman, 1989), p. 17.
9 Haffenden, John, *Viewpoints: Poets in Conversation* (London: Faber and Faber, 1981), p. 127.

to the impersonality of Symbolism and 'to the Symbolist poets of Europe' (*RW* 41), an important aspect of his work which has received critical attention chiefly from Andrew Motion[1] and Barbara Everett.[2] Larkin's desire for the self to be, in Keats's term, 'annihilated', to imagine 'the beauty of somewhere you're not,' finds its classic expression in the short poem 'Absences' from *The Less Deceived*. 'I suppose I like "Absences,"' Larkin wrote, 'because [...] I am always thrilled by the thought of what places look like when I am not there; [...] the last line, for instance, sounds like a slightly unconvincing translation from a French symbolist' (*FR* 17). Although Larkin said in his 'Introduction' to the reissue of *The North Ship* (1966) that his 'Celtic fever' abated when he discovered the poetry of Hardy in 1946, the division, as Andrew Motion has argued, is not so clear cut. Larkin's inclination towards Symbolism persisted from his Yeatsian phase through the English line of Hardy, more usually associated with him, and is to be found in such poems, in addition to 'Absences', as 'Next Please', 'Dry-Point' in *The Less Deceived*, 'Water' and the title poem in *The Whitsun Weddings* and, in the last collection, the title poem 'High Windows', 'Solar' and 'The Explosion'.

In his attempts to define it, Keats writes of the poetical Character as enabling the poet to lose his identity in that of others—'if a sparrow come before my window, I take part in its existence and pick about the gravel'[3]—distinguishing it from what he calls 'the Wordsworthian or "egotistical sublime."' Larkin disavows such Romantic egotism when he writes that 'The days when one could claim to be the priest of a mystery are gone' (*RW* 83). Yet despite his acknowledgement that the loss of self becomes the object of his longing for 'infinity, absence [...] somewhere you're not,' there is nevertheless a strong pressure of self-regard in Larkin's work which associates him very closely with the Romantic poets. Discussing Shelley in a radio programme in the 1970s, Christopher Ricks called him 'selfish as only the person who is deeply committed to the notion of selflessness can

---

1   Motion, Andrew, *Philip Larkin* (London, Methuen, 1982), pp. 72–83.
2   Everett, Barbara, 'Philip Larkin: After Symbolism' in *Essays in Criticism*, 30 (1980), pp. 227–42.
3   Letter to Bailey, 22 November, 1817.

be.'¹ In *A Defence of Poetry* Shelley writes that 'The great secret of morals is Love; or a going out of our own nature, and an identification of ourselves with the beautiful which exists in thought, action or person, not our own.' But this, Ricks comments, is a very dangerous way of putting it, 'because you find that you go out of yourself, but you go out into identifying yourself with everything else that exists; so that self which has been booted out of the door climbs back in through the window.' Tom Paulin describes how Larkin has in fact 'an altogether more ambitious concept of the poet that Milton, Shelley and Yeats would have approved' and sees him as being in direct line of descent from 'Milton's "high lonely tower" [...] Shelley's starlit "evening tower"' and 'Yeats's self-conscious recuperation of Milton and Shelley in *The Tower*.'² He cites examples from the poems, among them, the lines on Hull University Library, 'By day a lifted study-storehouse' and the 'tower symbol'³ of the lighthouse where its keeper cherishes his solitude in 'Livings II'. Distinguishing between the task of poet and novelist Larkin writes, 'if you tell a novelist "Life's not like that", he has to do something about it. The poet simply replies, "No, but I am."' (*RW* 96). This acknowledgement of the mimetic function of the novel and an insistence on the expressive 'I am' of the poet, recalls the assertive selfhood of John Clare's poem, 'I am', as well as the centrality of the poet's self-originating creative imagination, defined by Coleridge as 'a repetition in the finite mind of the eternal act of creation in the infinite I AM.'⁴ Thus the speaker in Larkin's 'Best Society' describes how, after locking his door and in the solitude of his room, 'there cautiously / Unfolds, emerges, what *I am*' (my emphasis).

Stephen Regan, however, argues that in a poem such as 'Here', Larkin's boundary between land and sea defines the limits of Romanticism and 'seriously questions the autonomy of the imagination and the transforming powers of "vision."' He calls it 'a decid-

---

1   The BBC was unable to provide me with a date of transmission for this mid-1970s programme: *Shelley: Unacknowledged Legislator*.

2   Paulin, Tom, 'Into the Heart of Englishness' in Regan, Stephen ed., *Philip Larkin* (Basingstoke: Palgrave Macmillan, 1997) 171–72.

3   Paulin, 173.

4   *Biographia Literaria*, Chapter 13.

edly *post-romantic* poem' in that the 'untalkative' existence pointed
to implies a freedom from language itself which, as language is
social, would indicate a condition that disqualifies poetry as having
any authority 'as a statement about the world.'[1]

Despite his aspirations towards the condition of transcendence
where language becomes inadequate to the task of expressing it, or is
imagined as disappearing altogether, it is true to say that, in popular
estimation, it is his notorious use of language with its various collo-
quialisms and crude forms of expression, which have made Larkin
'memorable.' The opening of 'This Be The Verse'[2] is now proba-
bly one of the most remembered and quoted lines of poetry in the
English language. '"They fuck you up" will clearly be my Lake Isle
of Innisfree,' wrote Larkin to Judy Egerton, 'I fully expect to hear it
recited by a thousand Girl Guides before I die' (*SL* 674).

The coarse idioms, the obscenities, which occur throughout the
poetry, have been described by Andrew Motion as 'a contemporary
and brutal version of the diction licensed by the Movement's rather
chummy democratic programme.'[3] And certainly the pragmatic dic-
tion which is the foundation of Larkin's poetry as a whole sits well
both with this assessment and with Larkin's own expressed concern
to re-route poetry which had gone off, as he said, 'on a loop line that
took it away from the general reader' (*RW* 216). Hence his dismissal
of what he called the '"myth-kitty" business' which handed poetry
over to the 'terribly educated' and the academics (*FR* 20) who have
'a professional interest in keeping poetry hard & full of allusions' (*SL*
307). For Larkin, to use classical and biblical mythology in the twen-
tieth-century was, he said, to fill poems 'full of dead spots' and to
dodge 'the writer's duty to be original'(*FR* 20). Here there are simi-
larities with Gerard Manley Hopkins's avoidance of what he called
'Parnassian' in poetry—'that is the language and style of poetry mas-
tered and at command but employed without any fresh inspiration.'[4]
Hopkins was a poet very much admired by Larkin who includes him,

---

1 Regan, Stephen, *Philip Larkin* (Basingstoke: Macmillan, 1992) 106.
2 'They fuck you up. Your mum and dad', *CP* 180.
3 Motion, Andrew, *Philip Larkin* (London: Methuen, 1982), p. 38.
4 Abbott, Claude Colleer ed., *The Correspondence of Gerard Manley Hopkins
   and Richard Watson Dixon* (London: Oxford University Press, 1935), p. 72.

along with Owen, Hardy and Edward Thomas, among those who have returned poetry to '"the principle that [it] is written by and for the whole man"' (*SL* 241) and who has 'clearly helped to form the twentieth century poet's consciousness' (*SL* 380). The influence of Hopkins's compound formations can be detected in Larkin's characteristic use of hyphenated compound words, 'car-tuning curt-haired sons', 'dog-breeding wool-defined women.'[1] However, there the similarity ends, if only in that the entire purpose of Hopkins's poetry, 'God to aggrandise, God to glorify'[2] would be denied in Larkin's conviction that belief in anything mythic or supernatural could not be supported. 'I am not interested,' he wrote, 'in things that aren't true' (*SL* 308). In this sense it may be that the sometimes crude language of the verse goes beyond what might simply be associated with the Movement's 'chummy democratic programme' and becomes symptomatic of a broader feeling of malaise. His poetry is often expressive of a sense of absurdity coming athwart the beauty, uniqueness and potential of human existence. With his heightened awareness of 'the solving emptiness / That lies just under all we do'[3] Larkin once again reveals close associations with some of the Romantic poets. A figure such as Byron, for example, speaks of Cain's crime against Abel as motivated, not by envy of his brother, but rather by his frustration at Abel's compliance with God's dispensation for him. Cain's act is an act of rebellion against the very human condition in which he finds himself. It is 'from rage and fury against the inadequacy of his state to his Conceptions—& which discharges itself rather against Life— and the author of Life —than the mere living.'[4] Larkin's obscenities and expletives may very well take their origin from a similar sense of frustration, and make up a form of metaphysical protest, no doubt shared by many, against that 'human condition in which he finds himself.'

Unlike Wordsworth, Larkin does not present his reader with a moral universe. In 'Next, Please', the justifiable (to us) demands we make

---

1   'Show Saturday', *CP* 199.
2   'The Candle Indoors'.
3   'Ambulances' *CP* 132.
4   Marchand, Leslie A., ed., *In the Wind's Eye: Byron's Letters and Journals* (London: John Murray, 1979) Vol. 9, p.54.

of life for reward—'all we are owed / For waiting so devoutly and so long' (18–19)—are met with what seems inevitable disappointment (10). 'We cry,' Larkin writes, 'Not only at exclusion'[1] from the past and because of our inability to inhabit what we are free to observe 'Rewarding others' (13),[2] but also at that past which 'leaves us free to cry.' It 'Won't call on us to justify / Our grief.'[3] The impotence of sorrow and our endless negotiation with an absence is its only bequest to us.

Philip Larkin was a very accomplished writer. As has been stated he was conscious of his gifts and took the business of being a poet extremely seriously. One of his greatest pleasures, if not the greatest of all, was jazz music. He could live for a day without poetry, he once said, but not for a single day without jazz. He possessed himself a modicum of musical ability (he played piano) and his ear for prosody, speech, timing, register would seem to owe something of a debt to his musical awareness and to jazz, about which he wrote authoritatively. A comparison might be made here with the American novelist, Ralph Ellison, who as a musician was able to transmit the rhythms and syncopations of jazz music into the prose structures of his masterpiece, *Invisible Man* (1953); or again with Hopkins whose working knowledge of musical notation and the principles of composition is transmitted to the musicality of his language. Donald Mitchell in an essay, 'Larkin's Music', describes how 'Love Songs in Age' is 'virtually through-composed, a continuity which erases the conventional strophic pattern and preserves unbroken the seamless rhythmic flow.'[4] Larkin's acute sense of musical form makes an important contribution to the structure of his verse.

Wordsworth, assuming the mantle of Milton whom he called 'my great predecessor', likened the body of his projected epic poem (*The Recluse*) to 'a gothic church' to which the 'preparatory poem' (*The Prelude*) would be a kind of 'ante-chapel' and all his other pieces the 'little cells, oratories, and sepulchral recesses ordinarily included

1   'Lines on a Young Lady's Photograph Album' *CP* 71.
2   'No Road' *CP* 47.
3   'Lines on a Young Lady's Photograph Album, stanza 7.
4   Mitchell, Donald, 'Larkin's Music' in Thwaite, Anthony ed., *Larkin at Sixty* (London: Faber, 1982) 79.

in those edifices.'¹ Perhaps with this in mind, Larkin told Anthony Thwaite that he 'would like to write a poem with such elaborate stanzas that one could wander round in them as in the aisles and side-chapels of some great cathedral.'² Not only does Larkin here seem characteristically to share Wordsworth's highly organised concepts of structure, but equally the sense of his own significance. That just as Wordsworth assumes a Miltonic stature for his intended epic poem, Larkin has a similar, if always discreetly reserved, consciousness of his own important relationship to his predecessors.

Larkin in September 1961
© The University of Hull

---

1   De Selincourt, Ernest and Darbishire, Helen eds., *The Poetical Works of William Wordsworth* (Oxford: Clarendon Press, 1949), Vol.5, 2.
2   Thwaite, Anthony, 'The Poetry of Philip Larkin' in Chambers, Harry ed., *Phoenix* 11/12, 1973–74, 51.

Part 3: Reading Selected Poems

3.1 From: *The Less Deceived* (1955)

Next, Please

'Next Please' anticipates the sinister summons, 'for now once more / The nurse beckons' of 'The Building' (50–51) where life is seen as no more than a waiting-room on our way to extinction. We are usually encouraged to get rid of the bad habits we pick up, but getting rid of 'bad habits of expectancy' will make no improvement to our circumstances. Eager short-term expectations are deceptive (a 'bluff', 5) in that when eventually our proverbial ship comes in it will bring not what we feel we are owed, but only that unavoidable 'something' which was 'always approaching'. The poem contrasts a shared sense of urgency to hasten time in our favour with the 'refusal' of an indifferent order of time to 'make haste'. The slow progress of this 'ship of plenty' anticipates the 'steamer stuck in the afternoon' in 'To the Sea'. The sense of time-present (stanza 4) fleetingly situated between our hopes of time-future and longings for time-past might be compared with the temporal dilemma presented in 'Triple Time'.

This comparatively brief six-stanza poem comprises a survey of the whole of life's inexorable advance to death from the time of conception and birth, implicit in 'expectancy' (2), 'big' [with child] (11), 'tits' (13), 'breed' and the breaking of waters (24).

Toads

In an address (August 16, 1837) 'The Commercial Spirit of Modern Times', the American writer Henry David Thoreau argued that:

> the order of things should be somewhat reversed; the seventh

should be man's day of toil, wherein to earn his living by the sweat of his brow; and the other six his Sabbath of the affections and the soul—in which to range this widespread garden, and drink in the soft influences and sublime revelations of Nature.[1]

Thoreau's words highlight the dilemma of the narrator of 'Toads' whose opening remark combines an indignant petulance—'Why *should* I?'—with a self-assertion marking him off from the common lot of man, 'Why should *I*?' (my emphases). Stanzas 3, 4 and 5, however, progressively weaken his argument even while it is in the process of being made. Staying just this side of poverty ('They don't end as paupers') and starvation ('No one actually *starves*') is not what might be called a recommendation for a life that Thoreau envisages being open to the 'soft influences and sublime revelations of Nature'.

The eating of windfalls (stanza 4) in a poem about work inevitably carries overtones of Eve's apple and the primal curse. But it is, of course, effort and education which have enabled this narrator to construct within the poem an allusive relationship between the colloquialism, 'Stuff your pension!' and 'that's the stuff / That dreams are made on' (23–24), a phrase recalling Prospero's 'We are such stuff / As dreams are made on' in *The Tempest*.[2] Work is an issue at the heart of that play where Gonzalo's dream of presiding over a regained golden age, with all men 'idle',[3] is at one extreme from the ethic of the hard work underlying the prosperity of Prospero's island in the first place. Larkin's slackly alliterative list of the workshy, 'Lecturers, lispers, / Losels, loblolly-men, louts' (10–11) reflects dubiously on those who live by their wits alone and implies the same kind of Devil-may-care attitude to be found in the fallen Eve's advice to the as yet unfallen Adam, 'fear of death deliver to the winds.'[4]

Despite his emphatic 'Why should *I*?', the narrator comes to acknowledge that he, too, shares the common lot, thus answering

---

1 Thoreau, H. D., *Early Essays and Miscellanies*, Moldenhauer, Joseph, J., Moser, Edwin, with Kern, Alexander (Princeton: Princeton University Press, MCMLXXV), p.117

2 *The Tempest*, 4.1.156–57.

3 *The Tempest* 2.1.155.

4 Milton, *Paradise Lost*, 9, 999.

for himself the questions posed in stanza 1. At the same time, he acknowledges the enduring attraction of a work-free society. The opening of the poem, 'Why should I let the toad *work* / Squat on my life' makes allusion to Milton's Satan, 'Squat like a toad, close at the ear of Eve'[1]— the beginning of a temptation which led to her fall and made work, as a consequence, her unavoidable legacy to our world ('In the sweat of thy face shalt thou eat bread').

Triple Time

The unremarkable present, a time with which we are never content, was once an eagerly anticipated future, full of the promises and potential of adult enterprise, and gently playing upon our air of expectancy as a 'lambent' flame plays upon a surface. This was a future 'heard in contending bells' (9), as the village 'bells', to the child Coleridge in 'Frost at Midnight', were 'like articulate sounds of things to come!'[2] And by the same token, time-present will shortly become 'the past', equally longed-for as that irrecoverable period where we now, in retrospect, seem to have wasted our opportunities.

The theme of 'deception' haunts about the poem's title (as it is of course implicit in the title of the collection). 'Double-time' brings to mind 'two timing'. And so here, as its victims, we've been not only, as it were, 'two-timed' but *three-timed*—'fleeced' by our chances which are imaged as lambs (implied in 'lambent'?), now grown into sheep, getting fat on things which, at the time, we unwittingly neglected to exploit to our own advantage.

'Double time' carries also the meaning of double the wages for working overtime. 'Triple Time' implies the promise, therefore, of even greater remuneration, except that the speed of time (to go at 'triple-time' being to go more swiftly even than at 'double-time') has brought us already to the end of our days, leaving us with, instead of an ample reward or 'increase', simply the 'threadbare' prospects of what remains to us—a 'seasonal decrease'. In fact, although it appears that time ensured that we were never really given a chance

---

1   *Paradise Lost*, 4, 800.
2   S. T. Coleridge, 'Frost at Midnight', 33.

(as in the idiomatic 'fat chance'—see line 12), we are always left annoyingly with the troubling thought that by acting differently we might have been happier. We blame on time, therefore, our own failures for not having acted otherwise than we did.

Evidence that this frustrating experience has always been a shared one can be seen in some lines of the eighteenth-century poet, John Dyer's *Grongar Hill* (1726) which are close to Larkin's; (Dyer's most celebrated poem, interestingly is called *The Fleece*—see 'Triple Time' 13):

> So we mistake the Future's face,
> Ey'd thro' Hope's deluding Glass;
> As yon Summit's soft and fair,
> Clad in Colours of the Air,
> Which to those who journey near,
> Barren, and brown, and rough appear;
> Still we tread tir'd the same coarse Way.
> The present's still a cloudy Day.' (121–28)

In a letter to Maeve Brennan, Larkin attempts to address the dilemma. 'I don't feel that everything could have been different if only I'd acted differently', he writes; 'to have acted differently I shd have needed to have *felt* differently, to have *been different*, wch means going back years and years, out of my lifetime' (*SL* 344).

No Road

As long as life endures it is always possible for two people who have agreed to sever their relationship to meet up again. The path between them, still visible beneath the overgrowth of the years, can always, if desired, be re-opened. Larkin admired a poem by Frances Cornford, 'All Souls' Night,[1] which he included in his *Oxford Book of Twentieth Century English Verse*. It describes just such a reunion, in this case of former lovers:

---

1 Frances Cornford (1886–1960). And see Brennan, Maeve, *The Philip Larkin I Knew* (Manchester: Manchester University Press, 2002), p. 47.

> My love came back to me
> Under the November tree
> Shelterless and dim.
> He put his hand upon my shoulder,
> He did not think me strange or older,
> Nor I, him.

Larkin's poem, however, promises no consolation of this kind. Instead, it anticipates time's victorious obliteration, in the long run, of all traces of the past, while at the same time designing a new world for others to live in, in which the one-time possibility of reunions for those in former relationships will have vanished without trace. The narrator's response is complex. He acknowledges that being free to watch the inevitability of this process, as though he were watching a cold sun rising to reward others, is a strange kind of 'liberty' (see the conclusion of 'Sad Steps'). On the other hand, it seems that having no wish to prevent it, in fact his even perversely *willing* it to happen, is to make himself the very source of his unhappiness.

Poetry of Departures

The title implies the artifice behind the pastoral impulse. Pastoral, the oldest of the genres, lends a kind of 'poetry' to the idea of departure, just as when we might refer to the 'poetry' of trees, or the 'poetry' of a dancer's movement.[1] As 'pastoral' was no more than the invention of witty and sophisticated writers comparing their urban societies with what they imagine to have been a better, rural existence, it has never reflected reality. Thus, no-one encounters persons who have actually abandoned everyday employment to live the 'idyllic' life of shepherds or gypsies or pirates. We only ever hear of them at five removes ('fifth-hand'). The epitaphic finality of 'He chucked up everything / And just cleared off' (3–4), dying to one form life in

---

1   A. T. Tolley says that the title is a translation of the phrase 'poésie des départs', 'a particular style of French nineteenth-century poem[...] in which the poet contemplates leaving the everyday world for a more romantic setting.' Tolley, A.T., *My Proper Ground: A Study of the Work of Philip Larkin and its Development* (Edinburgh: Edinburgh University Press, 1991), p. 76.

order to be reborn into another, is to be found only in books, where figures like Ishmael take to the ship ('This is my substitute for pistol and ball'[1]) or Huckleberry Finn to his raft, after first of course staging his own symbolic 'death'.[2]

A statement such as, '"*He walked out on the whole crowd*"' recalls Larkin's '"*Stuff your pension!*"' in 'Toads'; '"*Take that you bastard*"' anticipates 'the old right hook' in 'A Study of Reading Habits', a poem equally concerned with the inadequacy of fiction in the face of real life. The persistent relevance of pastoral to the human condition is that it makes possible the sober industriousness of maturity. Pastoral is as much an artificial creation as books, china and all the other 'specially-chosen junk' of the speaker's mundane life 'in perfect order'. To attempt to pursue it into reality, however, would be to abandon maturity in a reprehensible, because regressive, quest for an unobtainable idea of perfection.

Shakespeare's rationalist city-dweller, Duke Theseus in *A Midsummer Night's Dream*, expresses a rejection of what he regards as the regressive 'fables' and 'fairy toys' of the pastoral story he has been told.[3] For him, the obverse of his 'life in perfect order' would be that 'Reprehensibly perfect' one (32) involving a departure from 'cool reason'.[4] It is an alluring dream life to be found only in the poetry of departures, as Bottom's dream can be expressed, as he himself tells us, only in the form of poetry —'I will get Peter Quince to write a / Ballet [ballad] of this dream.'[5]

Dry-Point

This poem is one of a pair entitled 'Two Portraits of Sex' which appeared in Larkin's collection, *XX Poems* (April 1951) under the titles '1, Oils' and 'II, Etching'. The latter, with its punning title ('Itching'), was included in *The Less Deceived* as 'Dry-Point'. Dry-Point is a particularly delicate form of etching produced, as in all

---

1   Herman Melville, *Moby Dick*'', Chapter One.
2   Mark Twain, *Huckleberry Finn*, Chapter Seven.
3   *A Midsummer Night's Dream*, 5.1.3
4   *A Midsummer Night's Dream*, 5.1.6
5   *A Midsummer Night's Dream*, 4.1.214–15

such processes, by the use of a tool, but a process involving no fluids where other similar techniques might, for example, use an 'irritant' like acid. The poem takes Dry-Point as metaphor, with sex as the 'time-honoured irritant', describing what for the male participant in the sexual act is the dry point reached after the 'wet spark comes'. There may be a glance here at that 'imagined' electrical spark passing at the moment of creation between Adam's outstretched finger and the finger of God in Michelangelo's famous painting in the Sistine Chapel.[1]

In interview Larkin described how the poem was a way of saying 'how awful sex is and how we want to get away from it' (*FR* 51). 'Dry-Point certainly describes the sexual impulse as a troublesome recurrence demanding fulfilment 'until we begin dying'—that is, either 'Endlessly' (1) until death, or perhaps taking the Elizabethan use of the term 'dying' for the sexual act itself, a bursting of that particular 'bubble' (2). The experience of the rapist in Larkin's 'Deceptions', with his 'burst into fulfilment's desolate attic' (17), is one, it seems, universally shared. The magical promise of sexual delight is betrayed in the 'tristesse' of completion as the 'leaden' aspect of a 'ring' (9) reveals it to be an alloy, a cheap manufacture of 'Birmingham' (12) with its apparent reputation for the production of tawdry jewellery.

Sex is presented as a 'time-honoured' (1) reminder of our creaturely status. Despite our 'dream' (16) of a platonic existence from which the 'real' (7) physicality of sex is excluded, we have nevertheless to come to terms with our 'Bestial' (7) selves. In Sonnet 116, 'Let me not to the marriage of true minds / Admit impediments', Shakespeare takes 'impediments' in its Latin sense of 'impedimenta' or 'baggage.' The impedimenta of our minds are our bodies which we carry around with us—our 'depreciating luggage', as Larkin puts it in 'Maiden Name' (21).[2] But the sonnet's opening statement suggests the importunate presence of our bodies, as it were, knocking at the door for admission, or *an* admission, that they are at least as important, or perhaps even *more* important than minds. Larkin's 'remote [...] bare and sunscrubbed room [...] / We neither define nor prove' (13/15)

---

1   http://www.teslasociety.com/art.htm
2   *CP* 101.

finds its counterpart in the 'star' of Shakespeare's sonnet 'whose worth's unknown although its height be taken'. Keats's 'heart high-sorrowful and cloy'd / A burning forehead and a parching tongue'[1] is reflected in Larkin's 'landscape' of the body (female body?) with its post-coital 'ashen hills' and 'salted shrunken lakes' (10). The 'intent' (7) pursuit of sexual satisfaction leaves us, as always, in a position remote from that 'Intensely far' (14) and untried spiritual condition imagined by Shelley as a star in an 'unascended heaven / Pinnacled dim in the intense inane.'[2] We are, as Larkin suggests, 'enclosed' (5) or trapped by what Shelley called the 'loathsome mask',[3] of our flesh, just as we are 'padlocked' (13) out from that Platonic 'cube of light' we can 'neither define nor prove' (14–15).[4]

Deceptions

Larkin originally called this poem 'The Less Deceived' but transferred the phrase to the title of his collection of 1955, modifying Ophelia's reply to Hamlet's denial that he ever loved her, 'I was the more deceived.'[5] 'Deceptions' refers to the experience of a Victorian prostitute whose story is told by the journalist, Henry Mayhew, in *London Labour and the London Poor* (1861) and with part of which Larkin prefaces his poem. She recalls how, as a sixteen year old and up from the country, she was deceived by a man who befriends her in the street, taken on a succession of nightly walks and finally seduced in a brothel after first being given some drugged coffee. In Mayhew's account the seduction is reported as a very gradual process, but Larkin makes the rape an aggressively urgent affair where the rapist's overwhelming 'Desire' (13) has him 'stumbling' and

---

1 'Ode on a Grecian Urn', ll.29–30.....
2 P. B. Shelley, *Prometheus Unbound*, 3.4.ll.203–4.
3 *Prometheus Unbound* 3.4.193.
4 Kenneth Clark's description of the lantern in Goya's painting, *The Third of May, 1808*, as 'a hard white cube' in contrast with the pathetic 'tattered shape of the [firing squad victim's] white shirt' makes the same kind of point. See Clark, Kenneth, *Looking at Pictures* (London: John Murray, 1960, 1972), p.127. See also Larkin's term, 'flattened cube of light' in his lines on Hull University Library, 'By day, a lifted study-storehouse', *CP* 220.
5 *Hamlet*, 3.1.118–19.

'breathless' (16) in quest of fulfilment, all of which contrasts with the 'unhurried' (8) aftermath of his victim's experience. The very public shame of, and consequences for, the 'ruined' maid in Victorian society is implicit in words and phrases such as 'Worry' (4), 'light, unanswerable and tall and wide' (6), 'Your mind lay open' (9) and 'out on that bed' (15). Although Larkin's sympathies lie entirely with the victim, he seems to recognise, as Blake in 'London', the hypocrisies of a society which disavows any form of sexual behaviour outside of marriage. The sense of genteel propriety in 'bridal London bows the other way' can be construed as a form of restraint, where the homophonic 'bridle' (cp. the restraining 'bridles' in 'At Grass' 30) brings to mind the alternative and prohibitive sense of 'ban' in Blake's lyric (7), leading to a consideration of how dead marriages ('Marriage hearse' 16) become responsible for the 'youthful Harlot's' (14) existence in the first place.

The speaker's historical distance from the events described in Mayhew does not destroy his identification with the girl's experience. The sensuality in line 2 ('Bitter and sharp') vividly foregrounds a physical and emotional pain ('scar', 7, 'knives', 9) close enough almost to be tasted (1). Suffering, endemic within human experience, makes it able to be shared with an immediacy irrespective of time ('Even so distant'). As Wordsworth's Oswald puts it: 'Suffering is permanent, obscure and dark, / And shares the nature of infinity.'[1] The 'exact' (12) nature of suffering which *can* be realised contrasts in 'Deceptions' with our own 'erratic' (13) attempts to 'read' the motivations of desire (13). In Larkin's poem the rapist's action results not in expected fulfilment but in, for him, a deception greater than that practised on his victim. Wordsworth's Oswald allows for this, too. 'Action is transitory,' he says, 'a step, a blow, / The motion of a muscle—this way or that— / 'Tis done, and in the after-vacancy / We wonder at ourselves like men betrayed.'[2]

Hence Larkin can understand human desire while sympathising with the suffering it sometimes causes. He is neither able to 'Console' (11) the girl literally ('if I could'), because 'Slums, years have buried

---

1   Wordsworth, *The Borderers*, 3.1. ll.1543–44.
2   Wordsworth, *The Borderers*, 3.1. ll.1539–42.

you' (10), nor adequately in that, given her experience, he simply wouldn't presume ('I would not dare' 10). Central to the poem's purpose is to demonstrate that though she 'would hardly care' (14), the victim was, in Larkin's albeit bleak assessment, the more 'fortunate' in being, of the two, the less deceived.

At Grass

Larkin focusses on the unknowable otherness of the superannuated racehorses. The position he adopts is similar to that in poems by two writers he greatly admired. In 'Snake', D. H. Lawrence despises the voices of his 'accursed human education' which have led him to offend against a natural order he finds beautiful and in which he yearns to participate. In 'The Darkling Thrush' Thomas Hardy speculates on the mysterious causes, seemingly privy to the bird, which allow it to sing ecstatically in a comfortless winter dusk.

In their celebrated days as 'Almanacked' (24) classic race winners Larkin's horses, like the ponies in 'Show Saturday' 'dragged to and fro for / Bewildering requirements' (37–38), have had their lives usurped and 'artificed' (11) by human agency. In stanza 1 the poet reflects on the two horses now so utterly reabsorbed into the natural world as to have become, in contrast with their former prominence, almost invisible. The language deliberately recalls their classic racehorse days. Thus the eye that can 'hardly pick them out' might once have required the assistance of the race-goers' 'fieldglasses' of line 27. The wind gently distressing tail and mane (3) recalls its once dynamic effect on horses in the full flight of the chase. 'The other' (5) placed in the role of the one-time racegoing spectator but only 'seeming to look on' (5) stands by the 'one' (4) which freely 'crops grass', no longer subject to the riding 'crop' of its jockey. The horses have reclaimed their own rightful place, being free to stand or move about at will (stanza 1) but essentially within a natural order which resists human intelligibility. They 'shake their heads' (20) but do so only in an apparent response to the poet's speculations, as the *distance* which separates them from his world (1) is existentially greater than that which was once used to calculate the extent of their winning places ('perhaps / Two dozen distances' 8). For them, now remote from the bright and colourful glamour of summer race meetings (12–14), 'Dusk brims the shadows' (20) and their 'shelter' is sought in 'the cold shade' (2), as inexplicable as 'the 'growing gloom' from which Hardy's song-thrush chooses to express its 'joy illimited'. Like Hardy, excluded from the hidden world of his song thrush, Larkin can only reflect on how the horses 'gallop for what must be joy' (26).

At one of its levels, therefore, 'At Grass' celebrates the alterity of the horses' existence. They have 'slipped' (given the slip to) their artificially imposed celebrity, turning from the 'littered grass' (16) of race meetings to their own 'unmolesting meadows' (23). At another level the elegiac mode of the poem takes grass, as in Larkin's 'Cut Grass'[1] and 'The Mower,'[2] in the biblical sense —'All flesh is grass.'[3] There is a hint of earthly corruption in the plague of flies in stanza 4 (19), while life itself is imaged as a fight or conflict in the various military usages, 'squadrons' (15), 'stand at ease' (25), 'fieldglass' (27). The 'faded inlay' (12) of commemorative text points up the ephemeral nature of all existence, as well as the illusory nature of fame where such 'faded' inscriptions are testimony to the failing attempts we all make to preserve our shared, brief histories. The horses 'names live' (24) recalls the yearly commemoration of the fallen of the World Wars at the Cenotaph in London's Whitehall, 'Their name liveth for evermore', while the poem's conception of life as both a fight and a race has its origins in *Ecclesiastes*, 'the race is not to the swift, nor the battle to the strong.'[4] This is a quotation actually given by Larkin to his character, Miller, in his short play, *Round the Point*.[5]

Society's inequalities, therefore, implicit in the 'Silks' and 'parasols' (13–14), the paraphernalia distinguishing the 'Sport of Kings' from the humble life of the 'groom' and stable lad (29), will be done away with by the levelling grass-cropper (4), death. Time, in Hotspur's words, 'that takes survey of all the world, / Must have a

---

1   *CP* 183.
2   *CP* 214.
3   Isaiah, 40.16.
4   *Ecclesiastes*, 9.11.
5   Booth, James, ed., *Trouble at Willow Gables and Other Fictions* (London: Faber, 2002), p. 475.

stop,'[1] acknowledged perhaps in Larkin's phrase 'stop-watch proph-esies' (28) and the 'stop-press columns' (18) (obituaries?) in which the 'long cry' (16) of life's story ultimately subsides.

Though in one sense freer at grass than in their illustrious careers, the horses nevertheless submit to 'bridles in the evening' (30). Although the 'groom's boy' who brings them represents an oncom-ing generation he is, for Larkin, no more than part of that remorseless (and tragic) cycle of death and re-birth, possessing only the qualified freedom which is shared by all creatures.

Church Going

The immemorial ritual (8) of church attendance as it slowly disap-pears, lends new significance to the phrase 'church 'going' and to the pronouncement from the lectern, 'Here endeth' (15). Lying, however, behind the speaker's irreverence in letting the door 'thud shut' (2), his affecting an ignorance about the age of the roof, and adopting a tone of casual indifference by referring to the 'holy end' (6) and its furnishings as 'brass and stuff' (5), is an informed knowledge in the use of a word like 'pyx' (16), as well as a residual 'awkward rever-ence' (9) and a compulsion, at least outwardly, to observe convention in the gesture of a donation (albeit with a 'foreign' coin).

The poem begins with a statement that might alert a reader famil-iar with Larkin's poetry—'Once I am sure'. The opening of stanza 3 marks a shift from action to reflection, and the tendency of the rest of the poem is to present its speaker as someone 'at a loss' (20). Certainty is thus replaced by wondering; wondering what to look for; wondering (21) what churches will be turned into; wondering (38) who will be the last to seek the church for the reason it was orig-inally built. The debunking register makes a brief reappearance in stanza 5 (42–43). Competing now with the speaker's own 'hunger in himself to be more serious' (60), it represents at this stage no more than a token willingness to be facetious, as the poem in its solemn progress comes to recognise as valid the church's role in human his-tory. To free ourselves from its influence, as the speaker has found, is

---

1   *1 Henry 4*, 5.4.82–83

as difficult as kicking a habit, alcohol ('bibber'), sex ('randy'), drugs ('addict'). And often people will find themselves 'gravitating' back to that 'habit' which church going instilled, not because, for them, the church's 'message' is true, necessarily, but because the 'cross of ground' which enshrines it (47) speaks to their mortal condition, making it a 'proper' (appropriate) place in which those who wish to be less deceived can gradually come to 'grow wise' (62).

3.2 From: *The Whitsun Weddings* (1964)

Days

Forty-one of the poem's forty-eight words are monosyllables, lending a deceptive simplicity to a poem which opens with a child-like question. In an earlier poem (1940) Larkin refers to a fact being 'plain as a child's demand: why / Is the sun red?'[1]; 'What are days for?' recalls those similar kinds of ostensibly simple, but actually unanswerable, queries of the very young. And it should be noted that the second line does not provide an answer to line one's question. The phrasing of line 4, 'Time and time over', reminds us not just of the repetitiveness of days, but equally of how one day it will be for each of us individually, 'time over'. The universal and imponderable question of line 6 with its faint air of desperation, leads to a 'solving', a word recalling the 'solving emptiness' in 'Ambulances'. It implies not simply a 'resolution' but a *dis*solving of being into non-being.

Barbara Pym, the novelist and a long-time correspondent of Larkin's, writes in a letter to him (18 March 1977), 'the doctor's surgery is crowded but the vicar's study is empty. And there could be a sort of rivalry between them when it comes to dealing with life's difficulties.'[2] It is possible that she may have had this poem in mind. Certainly the two running figures could be seen as participating in a race; one, perhaps, desperately trying to add a few more days to an expiring life; the other to despatch it to eternal life—to provide an

---

1   *EPJ* 111.
2   Holt, Hazel, and Pym, Hilary, *A Very Private Eye: The Diaries, Letters and Notebooks of Barbara Pym* (London: Panther, 1985), p. 415.

answer, in effect, to the question of line 6.

The difficulty of running over fields in long coats conjures up images of undignified, even comical, movement, displacing priest and doctor from the decorum of their usual environments and putting them on the same level as the rest of us. The urgency at that stage in each of our lives with no more days available to us will require just such an abandonment of propriety, with a priest or a doctor compromising their dignity in prioritising assistance. The priest's black cassock, the doctor's white gown symbolise the position we will all then occupy, with the chromatic familiarity of every day resolved to a monochromatic reality of light and dark, life and death and dramatised so effectively by Gerard Manley Hopkins in his poem 'Spelt from Sibyl's Leaves'. There the daily onset of night is a sobering reminder to us of how we will all ultimately have to confront, 'black, white; right, wrong.' Hopkins's poem goes beyond 'Days', warning of the eternal consequences of how we have lived in this world— 'reck but, mind / But these two; ware of a world where but these two tell, each off the other'.

Talking in Bed

The poem presents two people intimately havened, seemingly, from a world which is indifferent to them. Yet the phraseology throughout suggests a discomforting instability. Talking in bed, something that ought to be easy, becomes increasingly 'more difficult'; 'lying together' and being 'honest' (2/3) might be construed as 'lying' together and being therefore dishonest. The effect Larkin achieves here is similar to the effect of ambivalence and uncertainty Shakespeare can sometimes create, as in Sonnet 116 for example, where in the process of celebrating the *constancy* of a platonic love, his word-choice intrudes into that constancy elements of doubt: 'love is *not* love / Which *alters* when it *alteration* finds, / Or *bends* with the *remover* to *remove*' (my emphases). Thus Larkin presents intimacy in terms of 'distance' (9) and the litotes, 'not untrue' and 'not unkind' (12) fails to carry the assurance of 'true' and 'kind'. Not for one moment is the reader allowed to imagine that comfort or rest are achievable. The mind's 'incomplete unrest' undermines the common phrase 'a complete rest'. What is built up is built only to be dispersed (6). The semantics themselves are uncertain of reference. Is 'more and more' in line 4, for example, an adjectival phrase qualifying time, or an adverbial phrase describing how it passes? The essential solitude of the individual is a predominant concern of Larkin's, and the two people here lying together and who go back 'so far' (2) may, in this context, put us in mind of the two original 'liars', Adam and Eve. Like Larkin, Milton in *Paradise Lost*, accentuates the essential solitude of every individual when, at the end of his poem, his own intimate couple though 'hand in hand,' through Eden take their '*solitary* way' (my emphasis).[1] In fact the exile of man from his original pastoral condition to an urban one may be suggested in the 'dark towns' which 'heap up' menacingly in stanza 3, and where the sense of exclusion is emphasised in 'None of this cares for us' (8).

A Study of Reading Habits

The narrator presents himself as someone who from schooldays had used reading as a means of escape into various forms of fantasy. The situation described in stanza 1 recalls advertisements for body-building courses, common in the 1950s, inviting puny, underdeveloped men, humiliated in front of their girls by muscular bullies, to get their own back. The second stanza moves to a later stage of development, into the realms of the feral and the primitive, of vampire ('cloaks and fangs' 9) and caveman ('The women I clubbed' 11). Here sexual fantasy topples over into suggestions of cruelty and brutality, although the darker realities of life are still buttressed against by the legitimising medium of books. The term 'ripping times' (10), for example, belongs as much to the language of the schoolboy adventure story as to the real 'Evil' (8) of figures like Jack the Ripper and his ilk who, when observed from behind the security of 'inch-thick' (7) glass, become no more than a fictional 'lark' (8).

The dismissive remark at the beginning of the third stanza dispenses with the formality of the written grammar that might be asso-

---

1   *Paradise Lost*, 12. 649.

ciated with books. What the speaker now 'knows' about life reflects ironically on what he 'knew' in stanza 1 (4). The realities of sex and violence, his familiarity with unreliability and cowardliness, make *reading* about such things simply redundant. The title of the poem implies the kind of serious investigative study that might be undertaken by a sociologist, or perhaps a librarian like Larkin himself, for example. But the poem's irreverent dismissal of books is not the outcome the reader might have been led to expect from the author of such a study. The narrator appears to be saying that *all* books fall short; that under the circumstances it was perhaps no more worth a great poet like Milton ruining his eyes (3) in his quest to write a major literary work, than it has been for himself with his own history of less edifying and ambitious reading habits.

As Bad as a Mile

Invariably to fail in our aims begins to look less and less like bad luck, and more and more like something unavoidable, something to do with failure as endemic in the human condition. In fact failure can be traced to its source in the Garden of Eden at the beginning of history, which is where the poem concludes. Larkin takes the proverbial 'A miss is as good as a mile', changing only the word 'good' to 'Bad'. Eve's one act of disobedience in tasting the fateful fruit caused us to miss our entire prospect of happiness, changing our 'good' to 'bad' with the bite of an apple, and of which we are reminded in everything we do, whether it be something significant, or something as trivial as missing our aim when attempting to throw ('shied', 1) an apple core into a basket.

An Arundel Tomb

The touching 'detail' (15) 'thrown off (17) by the sculptor as peripheral to the establishment of their 'Latin names' has come to be the 'final blazon' of the earl and countess (40) and the focus of the poem. Present-day 'succeeding eyes' (23), unable to 'read' (24) the iconography of an historically remote period, have given to this 'sweet commissioned grace' (16) another significance. It is in this sense that the detail has been 'transfigured' (37) 'into / Untruth' (37–38), or at least been made to represent truth of a different, perhaps now more acceptable and accessible, kind.

A Keatsian oxymoron, 'sharp tender shock' (11) alerts us to Keats' presence later in the poem where the tomb, like the <u>Grecian Urn</u> of the Ode, gives rise to reflection on beauty, truth and the passing of time. The Ode's 'O Attic shape, fair attitude' is echoed in Larkin's 'Only an attitude remains' (36), although his concern is less with a reciprocity between beauty and truth than it is to do with issues surrounding truth itself. The intimate couple from 'Talking in Bed', who find it increasingly difficult to find words which are 'true', are discovered 'Lying together' (perhaps also in the sense of being untrue to each other), just as here the earl and countess, lying supine together, perpetuate a lie (2)—the lie that love survives—in the detail of their touching hands being set in stone ('lie in stone' 2). Even they would not have thought 'to lie so long' (13).

The final couplet of Shakespeare's Sonnet 116, itself concerned with constancy and 'alteration' in love, provides Larkin with his ultimate rhyme, 'prove / Love'. Shakespeare's 'If this be error and upon me proved / I never writ, nor no man ever loved', however, concludes a sonnet into which so much uncertainty has been introduced that the assertiveness of its opening—'Let me not to the marriage of true minds admit impediments'—is called at this stage seriously into question. The last line of 'An Arundel Tomb' carries the tonal assuredness of Shakespeare's opening, but it, too, comes to be undermined, not only when we come to understand that our contemporary 'reading' of the tomb's detail transfigures it into 'Untruth' (38), but also by Larkin's statement that what is 'proved' about our 'almost-instinct' is not in fact true, but '*almost* true' (my emphasis). The statement turns out to be no more than a sleight of hand, a rhetorical gesture in the manner of Keats's conclusion to *Ode on a Grecian Urn* where the silent eloquence of the urn evades, as Keats deliberately demonstrates, such clumsy attempts to articulate its 'message.' Any 'truth' which the Arundel tomb might possess equally evades, Larkin implies, such a neatly epigrammatic conclusion.

Toads Revisited

When asked about his daily routine in a 1982 interview, Larkin described it as 'Work all day', adding that his particular way of ignoring the passing of time was to make 'every day and every year exactly the same' (*RW* 58). 'Toads Revisited', whose title alludes to a literary tradition giving the 'revisited poem' a special kind of status (here 'Toads' in *The Less Deceived*), is about the almost ritualistic significance of 'the toad *work*' in giving us a form of dependable support within our regular activities, ('Give me your arm' 35). To some extent it helps us to ignore what is described in 'Vers de Société' as thoughts of 'other things' (34).

The speaker's implication here is that far from being remote from the experience of life's victims, 'one of the men / You meet of an afternoon' (9–10), he is in fact too close to them for comfort. Their being 'stupid or weak' (18) is not an assessment made from a position of perceived superiority, nor does the exclamatory imperative 'Think of being them!' invite him to indulge a comfortable distancing. Instead, it is obliging him (and us) to 'Think of being them' and, confronting our resemblance to them, face up to the uncomfortable realisation that it is only the daily obligation of work that comes between us and those unemployed whom we see 'Turning over their failures / By some bed of lobelias' (25–26). In 'Vers de Société' beyond the 'light' and comfort zone of the speaker's room stands an identical apprehension of 'failure' (35).

Mr Bleaney

The first nine lines of the poem to 'I'll take it', skilfully set up a dramatic situation between chattering landlady and the listening narrator who silently looks around Mr Bleaney's room while taking in its details. The room itself is a kind of malign version of Van Gogh's 'Bedroom at Arles'[1], 'Bed, upright chair' and so on. Like the 'handsomest hotel' to which a hospital is compared in 'The Building' (1), Mr Bleaney's bedsit is a place of transition. Whatever 'the Bodies'

---

1   http://www.vangoghgallery.com Search: 'Bedroom at Arles'.

may have been (motor-car body manufacturing?) his situation as an inhabitant of his own body until 'moved' is that in which we all find ourselves. Grinning (23) in his one 'hired box' (stanza 6) anticipates the grinning contents of the coffin, and the word 'gravy' (otherwise a gratuitous little detail in stanza 4) becomes appropriate here. It has an identical significance in Dickens's *Great Expectations*, a novel which begins with its hero, Pip, at the grave of his parents and for whom Joe Gargery, his surrogate father, repeatedly ladles gravy at the Christmas dinner of Chapter 4. The room's view of a landscape, 'Tussocky, littered', is reminiscent, too, of the desolate garden of Satis in that novel, while the name 'Bleaney' and the solitary circumstances of Mr Bleaney's life, recall possibly *Bleak House* and the disconsolate dwelling of Jo the crossing sweeper, Tom all Alone's.

Life, as the poem implies, is a matter of chance ('So it happens' 10) in which, although inhabiting individual 'Bodies', we are all inescapably involved with one another. The statement, 'I lie / Where Mr Bleaney lay' (10–11) prefigures a time when the narrator and Mr Bleaney will lie together in their shared destiny. Even in his absence (is he just away or is he dead?) Mr Bleaney is still, albeit irritatingly, linked to the narrator through his legacy of the 'jabbering set' (radio/television?) (14).

The last two stanzas constitute one lengthy sentence whose complex syntax acknowledges at once the possibility of the separateness of Mr Bleaney and the narrator, as well as their being indistinguishable. Although he *knows* Mr Bleaney's habits (stanza 4) and his 'yearly frame' (stanza 5) (from the landlady's gossip, presumably), **either** the narrator does *not* know (stanza 7) if, having such thoughts as himself, Mr Bleaney, too, stood, as he does, and watched the clouds; **or**, whether Mr Bleaney, like the narrator, stood and watched the clouds but with thoughts privy to himself and therefore *different* from those of the narrator. The comment 'how we live measures our own nature' (25) gives the narrator a discomforting sense that he and Mr Bleaney are identical. And therefore, as readers of the poem, we too are led to share the same sense of unease, if only in that we have been manoeuvred by Larkin into identifying ourselves with the narrator in his separateness from both Mr Bleaney and the landlady.

MCMXIV

The demonstrative pronoun, 'those' (1), suggests the scrutinising of a sepia photograph from the era of the First World War. The observation of the details—the line of young men waiting to enlist, and the urban setting, occupies the first two stanzas. The third and fourth stanzas divert attention from the 'photograph' to an imagined landscape and to the narrator's reflections on it, as well as to the implications of the historical date. The structure has some similarity with that of Keats's 'Ode on a Grecian Urn' where the poet's attention to the detail on the urn itself (stanzas 1–3) is diverted in the fourth stanza to an imagined 'little town' and from thence to reflection in stanza five on the passing of time and the subjects of beauty and truth. This is lent weight in that 'MCMXIV' was one of two of his poems chosen by Larkin for James Gibson's anthology, *Let the Poet Choose* (1973), and in connection with which he makes allusion in his commentary to Keats's ode. He states that his choice represents the two kinds of poem he believes he writes—the beautiful and the true: 'I have always believed that beauty is beauty, truth truth, that is not all ye know on earth nor all ye need to know, and I think a poem usually starts off either from the feeling 'How beautiful that is or from the feeling How true that is' (*FR* 39).[1]

'MCMXIV' takes the year of the war's outbreak as a significant point of transition from an age of innocence to one of tragic knowledge. The young men 'standing [...] patiently' are presented like cattle for the slaughter (cp. 'What passing bell for these who die as cattle?')[2] while the 'stretched' (3) out queues bring to mind not only stretchers for the wounded but also those on which the fallen will be stretched out, their holiday-mood 'Grinning' (7) now changed into the fixed grin of death.[3] The 'uneven' (1) lines remind us that Death the Leveller will soon make, in Robert Bridges' term, 'unevenness even',[4] with perhaps a glance at the lyrics 'The Long and the Short

---

1   Keats, 'Ode on a Grecian Urn', ll.49–50.
2   Wilfred Owen, 'Anthem for Doomed Youth'.
3   See Larkin's poem 'Chant' (1940) 'the streets are full of soldiers that are going to be dead', *EPJ* 86.
4   Robert Bridges, 'London Snow' (1890).

and the Tall' from Fred Godfrey's 'Bless 'em All' (1917), typical of the period's songs in which the horror of conflict was often overlaid with a breezy jocularity, and consistent here with the terrible misreading of enlistment as 'An August Bank Holiday lark' (8).

In such contexts the 'bleached [...] names' (9–10) take on the whiteness of bones and 'dark-clothed children' come to represent mourners for lost fathers. Stanza three's historical retrospection is a reminder of the long history of war, dating here from the time of the Norman Conquest ('Domesday lines' 20) and implying that, over the centuries, man has been the author of his own misery. By contrast, the beauty of the natural world is of its own order, indifferent ('not caring' 17) to man's destructive insanity, but unable wholly to conceal it. Thus 'The place-names all hazed over / With flowering grasses' have associations, perhaps, with those other names inscribed on the partially overgrown headstones of the dead in earlier conflicts. The poem invites us also to look beyond present strife to the future ('Domesday'—Day of Judgement), implying that humanity's suffering is a constant, just as, in his Ode, Keats anticipates that the Urn will speak its message to future generations 'in midst of other woe / Than ours' (47–48). Thus 'fields / Shadowing Domesday lines' (19–20) may indicate historical battlefields, while the silence of the wheat is 'restless' (21), suggesting the likelihood of that silence being once again disturbed by future warfare.

In a talk for the BBC Larkin spoke of the title's Roman numerals representing the year 1914 'as you might see it on a monument'.[1] They seem here to serve the same function as Owen's 'Dulce et Decorum est', namely the reality of war obscured on a monument or cenotaph by a sense of implicit 'nobility' in its classical representation. The 'innocence' whose passing Larkin remarks at the end of the poem implies an intelligence insufficiently awakened to the falsehood of such strategies. The poem becomes a commentary on the disappearance of innocence from this 'archaic' (6), 'uneven' (1) long-'Established' (10) world of 'crowns' (5), 'sovereigns' (11), children 'Called after kings and queens' (12–13), of divisions between the upper-class patrons of the cricket match ('The Oval') and the

---

1   *The Living Poet*, BBC Third Programme, 3 July, 1964, *FR* 85......

proletarian football crowd ('Villa Park'), of a ruling class in 'huge houses' segregated from servants in 'tiny rooms' (23) who are left in the 'dust' of their masters' 'limousines' (24). Here we are reminded not only of the dust of this most recent lost world, but also of the dust in which eventually everyone will be made equal.

In a letter to Barbara Pym Larkin, with characteristic insouciance, talked of being 'rather fond' of this poem, calling it a '"trick" poem, all one sentence & no main verb' (*SL* 367), and of how this 'was entirely accidental, not a piece of daring experimentalism' (*FR* 85). However, 'MCMXIV' contrives with great skill to register the passing of an age of innocence as taking place 'Without a word' (28). There is, for example, no sudden break between stanzas to mark such a transition. The pronounced sibilance lends a whispering, a sense of something happening or that happened, below the level of the immediately obvious or audible.

The conclusion is a reminder of the repercussions of war for 'thousands of marriages' (3) including a pathetic image of enlistees 'Leaving the gardens tidy'. This detail may have a broader function in the light of the subject as 'the men / Leaving the gardens' recalls the original man to leave a garden, replacing a 'tidy' or, as Blake would describe it, 'unorganised innocence', for the 'organised innocence' which 'dwells with wisdom, never with ignorance'.[1] The final prayer is that this wisdom be granted. That such blind innocence leading to so terrible a catastrophe might never be repeated—'Never such innocence again'.

Ambulances

An atmosphere of secrecy and the unspoken pervades the poem. 'Closed like confessionals' anticipates 'The Building'[2] where the sick arrive 'to confess that something has gone wrong' (stanza 4). The ambulances coming to rest 'at any kerb' (5) (cp. 'The Building': 'what keep drawing up / At the entrance are not taxis' 5–6) are like a visitation ('visited' 6) from the angel of death. The 'glances' (3)

---

1   Blake: Notes written on the pages of *The Four Zoas*.
2   *CP* 191.

they absorb suggest only a momentary awareness in those for whom the ordinary business of life is pressing and for whom an ambulance's progress through a city's streets seems to have no immediate relevance. The 'glance' also implies an apprehensive reluctance to look too closely, or to dwell on, even for the brief second it takes to register, 'the solving emptiness / That lies just under all we do'.[1] That ambulances 'thread' their way through cities is significant. We are reminded of each 'thread of life' cut suddenly by Atropos, third member of the Three Fates, perhaps implied here by the 'sudden shut of loss' when the ambulance doors have closed.

There is a kind of silent complicity in the traffic which parts to let the ambulance go by, reminiscent of 'a lamp / Winked to the guard' in Wilfred Owen's poem ('The Send-Off') about soldiers on a train being sent to their deaths in war. But those who share this complicity have no more immunity from the services of the ambulance than those whom the hospital has not yet claimed for itself in 'The Building' and who, in Larkin's ironic line, walk 'Out to the car park, free' (40). The women bystanders who instinctively sympathise with the 'Poor soul' (17) in the ambulance are made to 'whisper' what we, as readers, would prefer not to hear at all, that that distress which will one day become their 'own' (18) will become ours, too.

The Whitsun Weddings

Like Coleridge's ancient mariner heading on his journey 'south' (44) and fleeing 'southward aye' (50),[2] the narrator of 'The Whitsun Weddings' takes a 'slow and stopping curve southwards' (11) towards London. Both Larkin's and Coleridge's central figures are solitaries whose 'tale' is told in the context of a wedding or weddings. And the significance of weddings, as the symbol or type of order in society, is similar in both poems. Both, in their respective ways, represent extremes of climate and weather conditions. In both, the sun is very

---

1 The phrase 'just under' recalls that 'icy pond' which 'lurks under' the hop poles in Edmund Blunden's 'The Midnight Skaters', providing a 'thin and wan' surface on which skaters are invited to defy death 'and let him hate you through the glass'. For Larkin here life is no more than a kind of skating on thin ice.

2 S. T. Coleridge: 'The Rime of the Ancient Mariner' (*Sibylline Leaves*, 1817).

prominent. The bright sun of 'The Rime of Ancient Mariner' (see stanzas 7, 21, 24, 27, 41, 42, 43, 46) has its counterpart in Larkin's poem in 'Whitsun' (1), 'sunlit' (2), 'cushions hot' (4), 'blinding windscreens' (7), 'tall heat' (10), 'short-shadowed' (12), 'a hothouse flashed' (14), 'sun' (20), 'spread out in the sun' (62).

The most significant 'event' in Coleridge's poem is the shooting of the albatross, an inexplicable act of hostility towards nature, whose consequence is to separate the mariner from the whole of creation, plunging him into a lengthy period of purgatorial expiation. The Mariner becomes the cause not only of his own personal disaster, but inevitably that of the 'Four times fifty living men' (216) who are dependent upon him. No man is an island and Coleridge's poetry, within the ethos of the Romantic Movement as a whole, emphasises the fellowship, fraternity and interdependence of all human beings, as well as the reciprocal and indispensable relationship of humanity with the entire creation. In Larkin's poem the destructive arrow of Coleridge's mariner figure is transformed into a symbol of creativity and connection. The 'arrow' is mentioned in the poem's penultimate line as the narrator and wedding couples reach the destination to which they have all been 'aimed' (64). The pronoun is significant— 'There *we* were aimed' (my emphasis)—because the erstwhile solitary narrator now shares in the communal experience of the wedding couples; he is part of that similar 'goodly company' extending to 'Old men, and babes, and loving friends / And youths and maidens gay' (604, 608–9) in which Coleridge's mariner participates and by which his attainment to wisdom is defined (624).

That moment for the mariner at which his separateness is transformed into fellowship comes when he blesses 'unaware' the 'happy living things' of nature (287, 282) and falls into a deep sleep from which he awakes to find that 'it rained' (300). The 'arrow shower [...] becoming rain' (instruments of death changed into life-promoting water) in Larkin's poem carries the same implications for its narrator's 'salvation'. In Coleridge's poem the awakening is an epiphany reflected in that similar moment of conversion at which Larkin's detached narrator 'Struck' (with its suggestion of an arrow, 29) makes connection with what he had hitherto disregarded or, at best, half noticed.

The arrow of course has traditionally been a symbol of sexuality and of creativity. One thinks of Blake's 'arrows of desire', and there are many such symbols and suggestions of sexuality and fertility in Larkin's poem—the ejaculatory 'gouts of steam' (51), the 'poplars' (52), the 'tower' (58), '[...] swelled [...] falling (70–71), and the 'squares of wheat' (63). The girls of the wedding parties stare at the departing couples as 'At a religious wounding' (49) bringing to mind perhaps Bernini's sculpture, 'The Ecstasy of St Teresa'[1] (1652) where the angel's spear/arrow and the swooning expression and languid pose of the saint point up a situation essentially spiritual but one which is filled with erotic intensity.

'The Whitsun Weddings' progresses from the heat of the sun, already noted, to suggestions of a more temperate climate, through 'shadows' (53) and 'cooling' (58) to 'rain' (72). Although, in context, notions of hope and fertility are implicit in the final stanza's 'arrow shower [...] becoming rain' (cp. Hopkins's Christ as 'A released shower, let flash to the shire' i.e. Essex, a county adjacent to London),[2] Larkin's poem also uses ideas of 'cooling' to indicate the Coleridgean frigidity and hopelessness of the life lived, and as Wordsworth puts it, 'at distance from the kind'.[3] Where Bernini's St Teresa is an emblem of both desire and deprivation, Larkin's 'walls of blackened moss' (65) are meant to bring to mind Tennyson's 'Mariana',[4] another tale of loneliness, hopeless longing and sexual frustration, imaged memorably in Millais' painting.[5] Larkin clearly intends the allusion, as elsewhere he makes use of Tennyson's word, 'knots',[6] (64) which implies both 'to tie the marriage knot', and the broken 'virgin knot' of a bride's first sexual encounter. The 'shadow of the poplar' which falls 'Upon [Mariana's] bed' (55–56), as a teasing image of the sex she is denied, is present in 'The Whitsun Weddings' where poplars 'cast / Long shadows' (53) over major roads.

---

1   http://upload.wikimedia.org/wikipedia/commons/4/4c/Ecstasy_St_Theresa_SM_della_Vittoria.jpg
2   *The Wreck of the Deutschland*, l.272.
3   *Elegiac Stanzas*, ll.53–54.
4   'Mariana' begins, 'With blackened moss'..
5   http://www.tate.org.uk Search: Millais 'Mariana'.
6   'The rusted nails fell from the knots / That held the pear to the gable wall', *Mariana*, ll. 3–4.

As often in Larkin the joyfulness of marriage is haunted by the omnipresence of the funereal. A poem about sex is also a poem about death. It has an 'interest' in 'what's happening in the shade' (21). Just as Coleridge's white albatross (Latin *alba* = white) gives way at one point to the horrifying 'death' figure of the encountered ship, so the obverse of Larkin's 'Whitsun' weddings (Whit–white) are those shadows which reduce the chromatic constituents of our lives, 'The lemons, mauves, and orange-ochres' (36) to the monochromatic choice confronting us at death, a choice between black and white (see 'Days'). In a theological context (Whitsun is Pentecost, the descent of the Holy Spirit), our choice is between the life of the spirit and the death of the soul. In Larkin's secular vision, our choice is between the 'death' of solitude and the 'life' of relationship. Again the southwards direction of the narrator's journey takes on significance. In Keats's 'The Eve of St Agnes', another poem about sexual desire and cold denial, Madeleine and her lover, Porphyro, escape to the home he has made for her 'o'er the southern moors' (351). It is the castle's ancient beadsman who 'Northward [...] turneth' (19) towards isolation and a world of 'icy hoods and mails' (18). 'The Whitsun Weddings', however, reminds us that we are never, even at the most joyful moments of our lives, free from thoughts of death. The ancient mariner is ultimately a 'sadder' *because* a 'wiser man', while Larkin's joyful 'Free at last' (45) is immediately made ironic (cp 'Out to the car park, free')[1] by the heavy register of the line which follows—'And loaded with the sum of all they saw.'

Dockery and Son

Larkin called this poem 'as true as anything I've ever written' (*FR* 49) and seems to have taken the idea of the return of a former student to his old college from a novel he admired called *The Senior Commoner* (1933) by Julian Hall. He quotes a passage from the novel in a 1982 article where he is writing about it: '"Junior to you, am I? But you've got a boy or a grandson or something at the place now. I haven't. I haven't got anybody"' (*RW* 277).

---

1   'The Building', l.40.

The poem opens with its speaker, formally dressed for the occasion and presented as a form of harbinger, a 'Death-suited' (3) revenant, whose presence as 'visitant' matches the 'memento mori' theme of the lines which follow. He discovers from the Dean that Dockery was his junior and, learning that Dockery's son is currently at the college, is led to reflect on time's passage and the divergence of individual lives. The 'Joining' and 'parting' railway lines (24) symbolise how his own life and Dockery's had once intersected and then diverged from each other. Larkin skilfully expresses the ramifications of his speaker's thought processes as they develop away from the cinematic fading of the Dean's voice in line 4 to the point where they are abandoned in sleep seventeen lines later. Ultimately, the speaker concludes, there is really no difference between himself and Dockery, in that what led Dockery to marriage and fatherhood was as 'Innate' (36) to him as 'To have no son, no wife' was, and still is, 'natural' for the speaker himself (25–26).

But what of course compounds their similarity is their shared subjugation to the inexorable ticking of the clock. The poem's title recalls the nursery rhyme, 'Hickory, Dickory, dock'[1] and time is marked in the poem by the college clock whose 'known bell chimes' the passing of the hours in line 10. The immediately preceding lines, recalling the speaker's wilder days of youth when required with his fellow students to 'give / Our version' of 'these incidents last night' (6–7), are meant perhaps to bring to mind Falstaff's 'chimes at midnight'.[2]

Shakespeare may be present in other significant ways. The words of the Player King in *Hamlet*, for example, 'Our thoughts are ours, their ends none of our own'[3] are similar to those in 'Dockery and Son' describing how in life we are left 'what something hidden from us chose' (47), while the speaker's inheritance—'Nothing with all a son's harsh patronage' (49)—recalls the significance of 'nothing' in *King Lear*, the harsh legacy of the son, Edmund, to his father,

---

1   In a letter to J. B. Sutton Larkin describes an 'absurd' variation on this nursery rhyme which obtruded on his mind 'preventing deeper thought', *SL* 98).

2   *2 Henry 4*, 3.2.215

3   *Hamlet*, 3.2.213

Gloucester.[1] Words here with sexual implications 'harden', 'got' (begot, 40), 'rear' (41), 'embodying' (42) find a counterpart in Edmund's sexualised language, 'I grow, I prosper; now, gods, stand up',[2] and are used to distinguish Dockery's sexually productive life from that of the 'unproductive' speaker.

'Nothing' stands also at one end of the scale of commodity. And in this sense the poem's title, recalling Dickens's *Dombey and Son*, shares that novel's sense of the ephemeral worth of possessions. Mr Dombey's hopes for his business to be carried on by his son, Paul, are dashed when Paul dies, and the ruminations of the poem's speaker about Dockery's taking 'stock / Of what he wanted' (30–31) inevitably bring to mind the son as 'stock' or breed, the inheritor of 'house' and 'land' (26) 'adding' (34) 'stock' to 'increase' (34) material wealth. In this connection the poem reminds us of the industrial north as the source of Victorian capitalism (so central an issue in Dickens's fiction) in 'the fumes / And furnace-glares of Sheffield' (20–21) where the speaker changes trains. Here a 'strong / Unhindered moon (24–25) presides, as it often does in the early industrial landscapes of painters like Joseph Wright, sometimes partially obscured, as in 'The Blacksmith's Shop',[3] to suggest the replacement of its 'poetical' light by the 'getting and spending' culture of industrialised society. In this poem the moonlight would be significantly fractured when reflected in the complicated configurations of the railway lines. But essentially, it is as a symbol of transience and instability that it appears in this poem. As Larkin's character John Kemp speculates in *Jill:* 'there was no difference between love fulfilled and love unfulfilled [...] What did it matter which road he took if they both led to the same place?'[4] For Dockery, his son *and* speaker alike, come boredom, fear, age 'and then the only end of age'.

---

1 John Osborne notes fifty recurrences of the word, 'nothing' in the *Collected Poems*. Osborne, John, *Larkin, Ideology and Critical Violence* (Basingstoke: Palgrave Macmillan, 2008), p. 253.
2 *King Lear*, 1.2.21–22
3 http://www.learnwithmuseums.org.uk Search: The Blacksmith's Shop – Joseph Wright
4 *Jill*, (London: Faber, 1985,), p. 243.

Self's the Man

The general consensus that the married Arnold lives less selfishly than the speaker himself, leads him to meet the implicit criticism by inviting the reader, ironically, to join it. However, in what follows, Arnold's life is so unenviably described (3–16) that by the time the statement is repeated (16) the reader is more likely to agree with the speaker's point of view; which might be summed up—'if this is what is meant by not being selfish, then I don't want to be 'unselfish'. The sexual sub-text subtly conveys a distinction between Arnold and speaker. Arnold, as a married man, has presumably ensured the sexual availability of his wife. On the other hand, it seems that Arnold's wife has replaced Arnold's masculinity by calling the shots herself. Instead of him 'screwing' her, she now orders *him* to 'Put a screw' in the wall (11). And although Arnold had been 'out for his own ends' (23) (in the sexual sense of ensuring he would 'have his end away'), he has now been obliged to surrender his manhood to a woman who's 'there all day' (4). The unmarried speaker of the poem, without the sexual opportunities of Arnold, has to rely upon his *self*, making do with what his 'hand' (29) can 'stand'. Yet it is this recourse to mas-turbation (traditionally, '*self*-abuse') which, it is wittily implied, goes some way to preserving the masculinity that Arnold has forfeited— ('Self's the Man').

Beneath the blunt colloquialisms, however, lie profounder reflec-tions on the nature of human experience. The speaker sees life as little more than a 'game' (27) for which, he argues himself into believing, he has not only 'a better hand' (sexually) than Arnold (29) but is also, as a free agent, likely to be a more successful player with the 'hand' life has dealt him. This statement, no sooner made, however, is char-acteristically undermined by self-doubt: 'Only I'm a better hand / At knowing what I can stand / Without them sending a van— / *Or I sup-pose I can*' (29–32)—(my emphasis).

Some sixteen years later, Larkin revisited this topic in his poem, 'The Life with a Hole in it',[1] in which he presents a speaker simi-larly accused of selfishness ('People [...] say *But you've always done*

---

1   *CP* 202.

what you want' 3) when he is compared to an Arnold-like 'spectacled schoolteaching sod / Six kids, and the wife in pod, / And her parents coming to stay' 14–16). Yet the opening statement of that poem, 'When I throw back my head and howl', implies the speaker's equally intolerable lot. As in 'Dockery and Son' where divergent paths lead speaker and subject to the same inevitable destination, the speaker of 'Self's the Man' decides of Arnold that 'he and I are the same' (28). The fate of both is to be carried away by a 'van' in whatever form it might take—ambulance/hearse?

'Self's the Man looks back to the ancient aphorism, 'nosce teipsum' ('know thyself'). 'Epistle II' of Pope's *Essay on Man* (1733) begins, 'Know then thyself, presume not God to scan / The proper study of mankind is man'. His opening lines go on to describe man's situation — 'in doubt to act, or rest; / In doubt to deem himself a god or beast; / In doubt his mind or body to prefer'. Implicit in Larkin's self-doubt, 'Or I suppose I can', is a lingering sense that if indeed 'Self's the Man', the speaker has somehow, in Pope's sense, failed to 'know himself'.

Larkin in April 1984
© The University of Hull

3.3 From: *High Windows* (1974)

To the Sea

Larkin works here with the same concepts of space and time as his famous predecessor in Hull, Andrew Marvell in 'To His Coy Mistress'. Marvell's opening line, 'Had we but world enough and time' involves geographical space separating the 'Ganges' (2) from the 'Humber' (7) and the unimaginable temporal extremities of 'ten years before the Flood' (4) and 'the conversion of the Jews' (10). Subsequent lines play variations on the space-time theme, 'Vaster than Empires, and more slow' (12), 'Desarts of vast Eternity' (24). Larkin similarly juxtaposes a spatial awareness, 'Sea' (title), 'further off' (8), 'sky' (13), 'enormous air' (15), 'distant' (25), against a temporal one, 'known long before' (3), 'afternoon' (9), 'as when' (19), 'farther back', (as against the spatial 'further off' 21), 'The white steamer has gone' (30).

In 'An Arundel Tomb', for example, the spatial/temporal juxtaposition is merged, in the line 'through lengths and breadths / Of time' (25–26). The 'sharp tender shock' (11), alerting in that poem the reader's attention to the casual detail of the joined hands, is echoed here in the view brought 'sharply back' (3). Not only is the scene brought 'sharply' into focus but it brings with it also the sharp poignancy felt by the poem's speaker ('Strange to it now' 23) when he sees that for others (cp. 'Sad Steps' 18) 'all of it' (10) 'plainly still occurs' (17).

The passage of time creates a perspective, making the one-time 'significance' of events, as Larkin says in 'Lines on a Young Lady's Photograph Album',[1] 'Smaller and clearer as the years go by' 45). It is not accidental that in 'Afternoons'[2] 'the albums, lettered / *Our Wedding*' should be lying 'Near the television' (14). The meaning of the word 'television' is to see things literally *at a distance*, and in 'To the Sea' the diminishing effect of things seen from the distance of maturity has reduced the seaside gaiety to something 'miniature' (4).

---

1   *CP* 71.
2   *CP* 121.

The poem is Wordsworthian in its vision of 'The still, sad music of humanity'.[1] All stages of life are represented; infancy ('the uncertain children, frilled in white' 14), childhood, courtship and marriage (stanza 3) and old age (16). Like Wordsworth, Larkin acknowledges that nothing can bring back those things lost to time. What Wordsworth calls those 'intimations of immortality' emanating from the perfect state from which through life we 'daily [...] travel', come to be replaced by the 'strength' found in 'years that bring the philosophic mind'.[2] For Larkin, too, the seaside's 'flawless weather' (32) is a reminder that we are not ourselves perfect ('flawless'), that our condition is a 'falling short' (32) of perfection. To keep our habitual (33), almost ritualistic, observances and abide by their standards is our only sure way of doing 'best' (33)—to 'Lead' (14) our children, to 'wheel' (15) the elderly, 'teaching' (35) and 'helping' (36). This is the moral vision of Wordsworth, made up of 'little, nameless, unremembered acts / Of kindness and of love'[3] and a vision realised here in Larkin's world of duties and social obligations.

Sad Steps

The narrator's are the 'sad steps' of advancing years, recalling the 'Palsied old step-takers' of 'Toads Revisited'. The crude colloquialism 'piss', in a context of such natural beauty and sublimity, accentuates the preposterousness (as it is seen) of the human situation, bringing it close to comedy ('laughable' 6). The narrator pays lip service, momentarily, to the kind of decorative imagery ('Lozenge of love! Medallion of Art!' 11) associated with the poetry of the Renaissance sonneteers, one of whom, Sir Philip Sidney, provides the inspiration for this poem.[4] The Romantic tradition is also brought to mind in the 'Stone-coloured light' sharpening the contours of the roofs (9). For

1   'Lines Composed a Few Miles above Tintern Abbey', l. 91.
2   'Ode: Intimations of Immortality from Recollections of Early Childhood', stanzas 5, 10.
3   'Tintern Abbey', ll. 34–35.
4   'With how sad steps, O Moon, thou climbst the skies!', Sonnet 31, *Astrophel and Stella*. Cp. Wordsworth's echo of this poem in *his* sonnet 'With how sad steps, O Moon...'.

Coleridge, idealising moonlight becomes a metaphor for the trans-forming power of the imagination modifying, as here, aspects of things without substantially changing them. But in the immediate context of the narrator's reflections, all such literary traditions are made to seem irrelevant. To dwell too much on the 'Immensements' (12)—time and space—is to turn oneself over to the 'wolves of memory!' (12) and be torn apart by them. Hence the shiver and aghast apprehension—'No'. Where Sidney found his 'lover's case' reciprocated in the 'sad steps' of the journeying moon, Larkin's speaker sees only a natural phenomenon, remote and unsympathetic ('High', 'separate' 10), whose hard, bright (14), 'wide stare' recalls Keats's 'Bright Star' keeping vigil 'with eternal lids apart' over the haunting brevity of our existence.

Vers de Société

Larkin was an instinctive avoider of social gatherings ('how I hate that word [party], as much as some people love it', *SL* 401)). His poem, 'Wants', anticipates this poem in its expression of a 'wish to be alone: however the sky grows dark with invitation-cards'. Vers de Société, a term for the light verse of upper-class social life, is here turned against the members it represents with their all too typically hyphenated names, and from one of whom the invitation has been received. The name for a male witch, (warlock), probably anticipates the pun contained in the 'bitch / Who's read nothing but *Which*'. The politesse of 'I'm afraid' (6) may therefore carry the additional implication of the speaker having the same fear of such gatherings as he would a ritual coven of male and female witches.

Over one hundred and sixty years earlier, in the first of his four 'Personal Talk' sonnets, and in lines which here anticipate Larkin's, Wordsworth proclaims his preference for solitude over society:

> I am not One who much or oft delight
> To season my fireside with personal talk,—
> Of friends, who live within an easy walk,
> Or neighbours, daily, weekly, in my sight:
> And, for my chance-acquaintance, ladies bright,

Sons, mothers, maidens withering on the stalk,
These all wear out of me, like Forms, with chalk
Painted on rich men's floors, for one feast night.
Better than such discourse doth silence long,
Long, barren silence, square with my desire;
To sit without emotion, hope, or aim,
In the loved presence of my cottage fire,
And listen to the flapping of the flame,
Or kettle whispering its faint undersong.

Larkin's speaker, although in the presence of his own 'breath-ing' gas fire he can understand, and to some degree celebrate, the rewards of Wordsworthian solitude ('repaid' 14), is nevertheless con-scious within it of the disturbing noise of the wind and the 'air-sharp-ened blade' of the moon, with their associations of transience and the scythe of time.[1] And, unlike Wordsworth, his conditioned unease suggests to him that '*All solitude is selfish*' (19). This leads on to an attempt to come to terms with the reasons behind the obligations we feel to be sociable, to take part in the rituals of boring small talk ('Asking that ass about his fool research'). The poem becomes a little exploratory at this point. It considers that perhaps because a belief in God no longer underpins the virtuous solitude once associated with the hermit, society has transferred its concept of virtue to sociabil-ity instead. Is this, therefore, the poem asks, like church-going, our simply pandering to a residual sense of 'goodness', to which we are still drawn but which carries no real conviction for us.

But here the poem abandons its speculations (cp. 'Arid interro-gation'),[2] and turns back to the voice of the fearful self. Only the young, it tells us, can live happily with solitude. As age comes on, solitude, like those similar moments 'when we are caught without / People or drink,'[3] brings 'Not peace', but (with a frightening inde-terminacy of expression) 'other things'. '*Dear Warlock-Williams:*

---

1 As early as 1943–44, in a poem 'Kick up the fire, and let the flames break loose', Larkin's speaker had asked, as a guest leaves at two in the morning, 'Who can confront the instantaneous grief of being alone?' *EPJ* 238.

2 'Aubade', l.8.

3 'Aubade', ll.36–37.

I'm afraid' therefore, in the initial and politely phrased inclination
to decline the invitation, provides a keynote for the poem as a whole
in its recognition of solitude as less and less inviting as our years go
by. Fear becomes the very reason the invitation is finally accepted:
'Dear Warlock-Williams: Why, of course' [implied: I'd be delighted
to come *because* 'I'm afraid' – see line 6].

The Building

Barbara Everett, in her essay 'Philip Larkin: After Symbolism', dis-
cussed the influence of Mallarmé's 'Les Fenêtres' on Larkin's poem,
'High Windows', and describes the influence on Mallarmé himself
of two prose–poems by Baudelaire, one of which begins, 'Cette vie
est un hôpital où chaque malade est possédé du désir de changer de
lit.'[1] Sir Thomas Browne in *Religio Medici* (1643) makes use of the
same image: 'For the world, I count it not an Inn, but a Hospital,
and a place, not to live, but to die in.'[2] Similarly, Larkin's hospital
'Building' is a pause on, and often a point of departure from, the jour-
ney we all make towards death. The few, therefore, who on this par-
ticular working day find themselves 'picked out of it' (28) sit tamely
on that journey as though on 'a local bus' (11). The building itself is
not the destination but, with its transient population, more like a kind
of 'hotel' (1)

The poem exploits our human apprehensions in the face of the
unfamiliar by describing things in terms more vaguely of what they
are not ('what keep drawing up / At the entrance are not taxis'). The
imagination is left, as in some Gothic novel, to make what it can of
rooms beyond doors 'and rooms past those, / And more rooms yet'
(24–25). What is being described here, though, is not fictional but
frighteningly real. Larkin is particularly effective in locating the spe-
cial taboos surrounding sickness, the secrecy in which it has to be
'confessed' (22), the sense people often have of something shameful,
or even sinful, about getting ill—'error' (23) that has to be admit-

---

1   'This life is a hospital in which every patient is consumed with the desire to
    change his bed'. See Everett, Barbara, 'Philip Larkin: After Symbolism' in Regan,
    Stephen ed., *Philip Larkin* (Basingstoke: Macmillan, 1997), p. 65.
2   *Religio Medici*, Pt 2. Sec. 2.

ted to a consultant as though to a priest in a confessional. He catches with unnerving accuracy the collective embarrassment in the self-conscious responses of those left in the waiting room as someone is taken off to an appointment (15–17). 'Ambulances' anticipates some of these particulars. The confessional box secrecy they suggest (1) by 'giving back / None of the glances they absorb' (2–3). The loosening of that 'unique random blend of families and fashions' (23–24) which looks ahead here to 'homes and names / Suddenly in abeyance' (18–19).

Lying 'beyond the stretch of any hand' and, for the hospital's patients, much more desirable, are not those things which are traditionally desirable because they transcend human life, but instead, and now made equally remote, those very ordinary activities of daily routine, kids chalking games, girls fetching their 'separates from the cleaners' (42–43). Larkin reverses Ernest Dowson's 'Out of a misty dream / Our path emerges for a while, then closes / Within a dream'[1] by describing life itself as the 'touching dream to which we all are lulled / But wake from separately' (46–47). In this sense, the girls' 'separates' take on a significance that could not have been anticipated, pointing to the very real 'separates' that as individuals we are.

The ever-growing hospital building seems to require the effort and enterprise once committed to the construction of churches. The activity within the building's 'lucent comb' (2) suggests the industriousness of bees in a hive',[2] its height the steeples or towers of cathedrals. However, this particular 'clean-sliced cliff' (a perilous brink on which people are poised between life and death), involves not a struggle to *ascend* but rather a struggle to *transcend* (my emphasis) the '*thought* of dying' (my emphasis) (61). It could be argued that in this respect the Church was *more* successful in its role. It was in itself a 'memento mori' with iconography obliging its flock to confront what, for a secular society, is perhaps the simply *un*thinkable. Enormous expense is involved ('how much money goes' 25) in what Larkin elsewhere refers to as 'The costly aversion of the eyes from

---

1 Ernest Dowson, 'Vitae summa brevis'.
2 See 'Honeycombs of houses, each / Its nervous cell of light and pity', *EPJ* 102

death'[1] The conclusion of the poem, therefore, with its suggestion that in attempting to contravene the 'coming dark' (63) the hospital is likely to be no more successful in its role than the Church has been invites this interesting comparison. What is inescapable, however, is the simple legacy of suffering and death; like a sigh breathed from the 'close-ribbed' (3), 'Red-brick' (39) back-to-backs of the Victorian period, to a high-tech, but no less vulnerable, present.

The concluding lines suggest the pathetic futility of bringing 'pro-pitiatory' gifts to the building when the dying are themselves the 'only coin / This place accepts' (56–57).

High Windows

The poem is a version of pastoral. It begins with 'a couple of kids' (the casual phrase in itself suggesting their slightly enviable irrespon-sibility) who are imagined by the speaker to be indulging the 'free love' that 'Everyone old has dreamed of all their lives' (5). 'Everyone old' includes not simply those in time-present who have reached old age, but those of previous generations for whom the pastoral ideal has always represented freedom from 'Bonds and gestures' (6) and the need to work for a living. As in 'Toads', where Larkin's dream of release from the primal curse of work ('the stuff / That dreams are made on') recalls Gonzalo's notion of a society 'Without sweat or endeavour',[2] Larkin's speaker in this poem imagines a world with-out 'sweating' (12), where the 'combine harvester' (7), a machine to alleviate the work of reaping (and symbolic of all attempts to render work easier), has itself been 'pushed to one side' (6) as 'out-dated' (7).[3] 'Free love' remains an ideal as much in Larkin's soci-ety as in Gonzalo's imagined one, cynically described by Antonio and Sebastian as a world where there would be 'No marrying' but 'all idle', all 'whores and knaves'.[4] The parallel phrasing in 'High

1   'Wants', l.9.
2   *The Tempest*, 2.1.161
3   Contrast Gonzalo's vision with the opening of Prospero's masque: 'certain Nymphs' address 'Reapers'—'You sunburn'd sicklemen of August weary', 4.1.134. Prospero's island is made productive by work.
4   *The Tempest*, 2.1.166–67

Windows' is suggesting that 'everyone young' (8) will inevitably dis-
cover with 'everyone old' (5) that 'paradise' (40) is beyond reach.
Hence the ironic remark, 'I know this is paradise' (4), and the sexual
overtones in 'going down the long slide to happiness' (8), implying
not so much erotic fulfilment as social and moral decline. The phrase
is echoed in the fourth stanza where 'the priest [...] / And his lot' are
like 'birds' going 'down the long slide' of freedom, an oddly incon-
gruous image, putting a serious question mark over the likelihood of
happiness or freedom ever being achieved.

The ideal is situated at the opposite end of this poem's vertical
scale —'beyond' (19) the confining 'glass' (18) of 'high windows'
(17) — in a realm of pure thought 'Rather than words' (17). The
sublime vista of the 'deep blue air' (19) is like the Shelleyan 'inane'
of *Prometheus Unbound*,[1] or the white 'vacancy' of 'Mont Blanc'[2]
which, instead of guaranteeing and protecting the idea of a deity, like
the view from high windows, shows 'Nothing' (20).

Show Saturday

The present indicative gives immediacy to the description as the
speaker takes in the spectacle of the annual event. A gentle reminder
of life's disappointments inhabits the opening remark—not a 'great'
day, as hoped, for the Show, but instead, a 'Grey day'. The 'Regenerate
union' (64) is as natural as vegetation which 'dies back' (58) stay-
ing 'hidden [...] below' (59) to burgeon again 'each year' (63). It
is an old, 'ancestrally' recurring process reflected in the 'recession
of skills' (32) found even in the simplest of its exhibits. Thus the
effect of the parenthetical remarks (3–4, 5, 6, 28, 29–30, 45–46) is to
convey a sense of familiarity. There are touching little observations,
'a beer-marquee that / Half screens a canvas Gents', or of the occa-
sionally unexpected, the victory of the grey-haired wrestler (21) or
the embroidery on the young wrestlers' tights (18–19). But overall,
there are no surprises here.

However, the comforting familiarity of the Show exists within a

---

1 *Prometheus Unbound*, 3.4.204
2 P. B. Shelley, 'Mont Blanc', l.144

much less comforting awareness of time's 'rolling smithy-smoke' (61), announcing a new order that is always in the process of being forged. The future, represented by the 'cars' in the 'narrow lanes' (1), the car parks (17), and the 'car-tuning curt-haired sons' (52) seems out of sympathy with the immemorial scene, perhaps justifying the anxious tone in the imprecatory conclusion, 'Let it always be there' (64). As in 'To the Sea', the process of time is coterminous with a spatial awareness as the cars give way to trees and then 'pale sky' (18). There are 'spaces / Not given to anything much' (14–15) and where (reminiscent of 'the unique random blend / Of families [...] loosen'[1]) families seem to disintegrate. The 'kids' are 'freed' (15) from parents (who are not to be their 'owners' for much longer) who 'stare different ways' (16).

The 'Regenerate union' (64), therefore, is illusory. It is like the 'baseless fabric' or 'insubstantial pageant' of Prospero's vision;[2] 'each scene' (14) makes up for its audience 'something they share' for a few hours, but whose 'shifting scenery' (39) leaving the 'dismantled Show' (57) is a reminder of a transience beneath the apparent stolidity. As often in Larkin's poetry, participation in such rituals serves as a replacement for, or secularisation of, the pieties associated with religious observances, and of which we are reminded here, for example, by 'blanch leeks' that stand in for 'church candles' (27).

Annus Mirabilis

The title is taken from John Dryden's poem (1667) in heroic stanzas celebrating a series of victorious English naval battles against the Dutch, as well as Charles II's projected reconstruction of London after the Great Fire of 1666. From the 'year of miracles' Dryden looks to a 'nobler city' who 'from her fires does rise', the symbol of a country whose wealth and power, it is to be expected, will come to be the envy of Europe and the world.

Larkin presents the England of 'nineteen sixty-three' (2) as no longer a country defined by virtues such as courage and loyalty, but

---

1   'Ambulances', ll.23–24.
2   *The Tempest*, 4.1.151, 155

one given over wholly to the pursuit of pleasure. 'Pleasure' is its beginning ('Sexual intercourse') and its end, 'Please, Please Me' ('the Beatles' first LP'). The speaker is placed within the historical process and implies that, in this new era, sexual pleasure had become more easily accessible through the relaxation of censorship ('the end of the *Chatterley* ban' 4) and the contemporaneous arrival (implied) of the contraceptive pill. In the general climate of popular culture, symbolised by the Beatles, the mores of the past were being called into question.

In Dryden's poem the 'dire contagion' of the fire of London 'spread so fast' that the old city was completely destroyed. In Larkin's, a new society has dispensed with those older attitudes to sexual behaviour which created a 'shame' (a roseate, incendiary blushing) that 'started' at 'sixteen' (9) and, like a fire, 'spread to everything' (9–10). Sex was made a commodity in the form of the 'bargaining' (7) and the wrangling 'for a ring' (8) which had had to take place before it became socially acceptable within marriage. But the new moral climate, Larkin's poem appears to be saying, has made sex no less a part of the economics of consumerism. In 'life was never better' (16) Larkin possibly echoes the famous remark of Harold Macmillan,[1] 'Most of our people have never had it so good'[2] which, in Larkin's context, is capable of a sexual construction, just as his 'brilliant breaking of the bank' links sex with money and may be read as a term for hitting the sexual jackpot.

In nineteen sixty-three, the socially constructed class divisions within English society (highlighted in the relationship between an aristocratic woman and working class male in *Lady Chatterley's Lover*)[3] were apparently dissolving in a demotic consensus—'Everyone felt the same'(12). Yet the telling word 'felt' implies here no more reliability than a gambler's conviction that his game is 'unlosable' (15). Thus

---

1 British Prime Minister, 1957–63.
2 Macmillan was, in turn, drawing on the US Democratic slogan of 1952, 'You've never had it so good'.
3 Mervyn Griffith-Jones, Chief Prosecutor at the 1960 obscenity trial, had asked if Lawrence's *Lady Chatterley's Lover* was the kind of book 'you would wish your wife or servants to read'. Penguin Books had been prosecuted for publishing the unexpurgated edition.

the opening statement of the last stanza is placed in an ironic light. Regret on the speaker's part at being excluded from all the fun is certainly carried in the wistful tone of the parenthetical voice (18). But the voice does not conceal an implication that a belief that life is only an affair of pleasure (a 'game' 15) is, in the light of Dryden's heroics, not only to trivialise it, but also to ignore the lesson of history— in Feste's words, 'pleasure will be paid, one time or another.'[1]

The Trees

The annual reawakening of the trees is more an occasion for 'grief' than for joy, recalling T. S. Eliot's 'April is the cruellest month'. The trees in their new apparel, 'Their yearly trick' (tricked out), carries the same sense of deception as 'bluff' in 'Next Please'. The triple repetition, 'afresh', in the final line effectively cancels the apparent optimism, as Macbeth's 'To-morrow, and to-morrow, and to-morrow'[2] conveys a weariness at odds with the 'promise' in the word (as, for example, Milton uses it—'Tomorrow to fresh woods, and pastures new').[3]

The poem is an attempt to interrogate the language of the natural world. The trees coming into leaf is 'Like something almost being said' (2), something even 'written down'(8), but somehow remaining teasingly elusive and excluding. There is a search to give expression to the felt reciprocity between human experience and the life of the trees, as a Romantic like Coleridge also searched for it.

> In looking at objects of Nature while I am thinking, as at yonder moon dim-glimmering thro' the dewy window-pane, I seem rather to be seeking, as it were *asking*, a symbolical language for something within me that already and forever exists [...].[4]

---

1   *Twelfth Night*, 2.4.70
2   *Macbeth*, 5.5.19
3   Milton, *Lycidas*.
4   Coburn, K. ed., *The Notebooks of Samuel Taylor Coleridge* (Princeton: 1957–2002), 5 Vols., 2, No.2546.

3.4 Valediction (*Times Literary Supplement*, 23 December 1977)

Aubade

'Aubade' was the last major poem to be published by Larkin. Its title is a term for a morning song (from French *aube* = 'dawn', from Latin *alba,* 'white') and it makes use, as in 'Days' and 'The Whitsun Weddings', of a light/dark motif. Its strategic appearance on the day before Christmas Eve, 1977, invites a comparison with Milton's 'Ode on the Morning of Christ's Nativity' (1629). Milton deploys multiple references to the approaching light of Christ the Saviour. He is, for example, the 'light insufferable' (8), the 'far-beaming blaze' (9), the 'Prince of light' (62), the 'greater sun' (83) arriving 'ere the point of dawn' (86) to dispel the representatives of pagan and infernal darkness listed in stanzas xxii–xxvi. Larkin's poem provides a very different version from Milton's Ode. Its speaker awakes at four in the morning to 'soundless dark'. In time 'the curtain edges will grow light' but, meanwhile, the thought of 'Unresting death' (5) is the 'glare' at which the mind 'blanks' (11). The 'realisation' (35) of its inevitability 'rages out / In furnace fear' (35–36) associated more with the 'dismal' company of Moloch and their 'furnace blue' in Milton's Ode (210).

Gradually the 'light strengthens' (41) but morning reveals 'no sun' (48), only a sky 'white as clay' (49), reminding us of the poem's speaker as Adamic man ('Adam' = 'earth') in his 'darksom House of mortal Clay' (Milton, 'Ode', 14). Here, however, there is no Christmas hope of a redemptive second Adam. Instead, the poem begins with the legacy of Adam's curse, 'I work all day', and ends with it—'Work has to be done' (34). This is the consequence of our 'wrong beginnings' (15), the subject, too, of 'As Bad as a Mile'. Thus the joy of Milton's 'Aubade' is destroyed in Larkin's poem by a cumulative deployment of negative constructions. They are: 'soundless', 'not in remorse', 'good not done', 'love not given', 'unused', 'never', 'emptiness', 'extinction', 'not be here', 'not to be anywhere', 'nothing more terrible', 'nothing more true', 'no sight', 'no sound', 'No touch', 'nothing', 'Nothing', 'none', 'unfocused', 'indecision', 'no good', 'not scaring', 'no one', 'can't escape', 'can't accept', 'no different', 'no sun'.

The speaker in 'Aubade' shares with Hamlet, in his famous soliloquy, the cast of mind which 'slows each impulse down to indecision' (33).[1] 'The anaesthetic from which none come round' has echoes of the 'undiscover'd country, from whose bourn / No traveller returns,' while the 'Not to be' construction (18–19) also suggests the connection. The fear expressed in the poem is closely akin to that of Claudio's with his speculations on death in *Measure for Measure*.[2] The physicality of a 'sensible warm motion' reduced to a lifeless 'kneaded clod' is reflected in Larkin's lines on the dread of that very loss of physicality (27–29). Larkin compounds a sense of unease by making the commonplace unfamiliar. In the dawn light of stanza 5, *something* 'takes shape' (41). For all the world like a horrible image from an M. R. James ghost story, a 'wardrobe' (42) 'stands plain' (as a coffin, perhaps?). In 'locked-up offices' (46) telephones 'getting ready to ring' (45) 'crouch' like predatory cats getting ready to spring. In sinister fashion, familiar 'postal rounds', like 'doctors' rounds', remind us daily that 'in the midst of life we are in death.'[3]

In 'Aubade' the divide between the familiar and our own extinction is shown to be tenuous in the extreme, while the syntactically separated, 'And soon' (20), reminds us that our prospect of crossing it is alarmingly close.

---

1   *Hamlet*, 3.1.83–87
2   *Measure for Measure*, 3.1.117–31
3   Book of Common Prayer, Burial service.

Part 4: Reception

Larkin's second published collection, *The Less Deceived,* had gone into its fifth impression by the end of 1957, establishing his reputation as one of the century's most important poets. The reviews ranged from those identifying a new and significant voice in a collection unequalled since the end of the war, to those which saw Larkin as representative of the Movement, returning poetry to accessibility from the obscurities of Modernism. Less favourable reviews included David Wright's in *Encounter* which saw Larkin as afflicted with the 'palsy of playing safe'[1] and a contribution to *Essays in Criticism* in 1957 entitled 'The Middle Brow Muse' by Charles Tomlinson. This piece was in fact a review of Robert Conquest's *New Lines* anthology of 1956 in which Tomlinson wrote of The Movement poets' 'singular want of vital awareness of the continuum outside themselves, of the mystery bodied over against them in the created universe, which they fail to experience with any degree of sharpness or to embody with any instress or sensuous depth.'

Accusing Larkin in particular of 'intense parochialism', Tomlinson collectively categorised the Movement poets as seldom for a moment escaping from beyond that suburban mental ratio' which they 'impose on their experience'.[2] Taking up a position wholly opposed to Tomlinson's, Robert Conquest in his Introduction to the second edition of *New Lines* in 1962 defended the anthology's poets, seeing in them a tendency towards 'a genuine and healthy poetry' (xi) which, he goes on to say, 'submits to no great systems of theoretical constructs nor agglomerations of unconscious commands' being 'free from both mystical and logical compulsions and [...] empirical in its attitude to all that comes' (xv).

---

1   Quoted in Bradford, Richard, *First Boredom, Then Fear: The Life of Philip Larkin* (London: Peter Owen, 2005) p.144.

2   Tomlinson, Charles, 'The Middle Brow Muse' in *Essays in Criticism*, Vol. vii, October, 1957, No. 4, p.460.

Conquest's description of a poetry working within the parameters of the empirical and approving of what Tomlinson picks out as a fault, namely an apparent lack of awareness 'of the mystery bodied over against them' and the imposition of a 'suburban mental ratio [...] on their experience', has very close parallels with the way in which Keats's poetry in his time, as well as that of his friend, Leigh Hunt, divided critical opinion. Although the kind of criticism from the likes of John Gibson Lockhart and Lord Byron was essentially predicated on issues of social divisiveness and class, the terminology employed was similar. Thus *Blackwood's Edinburgh Magazine* described Leigh Hunt, as the 'ideal of a Cockney Poet [...] altogether unacquainted with the face of nature in her magnificent scenes'. He 'raves perpetually about "green fields", "jaunty streams", and "o'erarching leafiness" exactly as a Cheapside shop-keeper does about the beauties of his box on the Camberwell road'.[1] For Byron, Keats 'took the wrong line as a poet—and was spoilt by Cockneyfying and Suburbing.'[2] Clearly, to a literary establishment whose tastes had been informed by the Romantic sublime, by the mysterious powers and enlargement of vision associated with Wordsworth, the poetry which reflected the tastes of a cultured middle-class was, in David Wright's phrase, 'playing safe'. The analogy with the Movement poets could be taken further, in the sense that the so-called 'suburbanism' of Keats and Hunt represented the emerging desire in the nineteenth-century for a post-war domestic and cultural stability, just as the poets of the 1950s emerging from the cataclysm of the war, it might be argued, reacted against the 'wild, loose emotion' of the neo-Romantics of the 1940s, represented by figures like Dylan Thomas. The phrase is taken from the essay, 'The New Poetry or Beyond the Gentility Principle', with which its editor, A. Alvarez, prefaced his 1962 anthology, *The New Poetry*. This was an important statement in which Alvarez surveyed the poetical output of the previous decades, assessing its characteristics and attempting to account for it. Thus the Modernist experimentalism of the 1920s had been superseded by the kind of poetry asso-

---

1   John Gibson Lockhart, 'On the Cockney School of Poetry'. *Blackwood's Edinburgh Magazine*, October, 1817, 39.
2   Letter to Murray, 26 April 1821. Marchand, Leslie, ed,, *Byron's Letters and Journals* (London: John Murray, 1978) Vol. 8, p.102.

ciated with Auden, the product of an age which, because 'the political situation was too urgent' had no time 'to be difficult or inward or experimental'. Auden had produced 'social, occasional verse, mostly traditional in form, but highly up-to-date in idiom'. The reaction to Auden had resulted in a 'form of anti-intellectualism' and the rhetorical work of figures like Dylan Thomas, whereas the Movement's reaction was 'in short, academic-administrative verse, polite, knowledgeable, efficient, polished, and, its quiet way, even intelligent'.

Of the nine poets to appear in *New Lines*, Alvarez points out that 'six, at the time, were university teachers, two librarians, and one a Civil Servant'. It was no surprise, therefore, that Conquest, as editor, could define the Movement's poetry in terms only of negatives, 'no great systems [...] free from [the] mystical' and so on. To illustrate his case, Alvarez constructs a twelve-line poem comprising no more than two lines from eight of the nine *New Lines* poets, producing tonally a 'kind of unity of flatness' which, he says, can be summed up by the beginning of Larkin's 'Church Going', 'Hatless, I take off / My cycle-clips in awkward reverence'. The figure depicted is what he calls 'the image of the post-war Welfare State Englishman: shabby and not concerned with his appearance; poor—he has a bike, not a car; gauche but full of agnostic piety; underfed, underpaid, overtaxed, hopeless, bored, wry'. This is another example of what, by this point in his essay, Alvarez has called 'negative feed-back' in poetry. Instead of the poet being an inspired 'strange' being, 'he is just like the man next door—in fact, he probably *is* the man next door.'

The critic Stephen Regan has raised objections to this assessment. As well as suggesting that Larkin's persona is perhaps more 'modern' than Alvarez allows, he asks why such ordinariness should be construed as negative, while also pointing out that Alvarez's remarks make no attempt to distinguish between poet and persona. [1] This is an issue which has bedevilled Larkin criticism, often to the poet's detriment, and will be returned to. It may be that in his composite list of the Welfare State Englishman's 'attributes', some may be applicable to the persona of 'Church Going', but the poem itself offers no evidence of its speaker as 'underfed, underpaid, overtaxed, hopeless'

---

1   Regan, Stephen, *Philip Larkin* (Basingstoke: Macmillan, 1992) p.28.

and so on. Yet for Alvarez, in the essay, the 'gentility' of the poetry under consideration reflects 'the idea that life in England goes on much as it always has [...] a belief that life is always more or less orderly, people always more or less polite, their emotions and habits more or less decent and more or less controllable; that God, in short, is more or less good.'

The argument then moves to a conclusion by declaring that England's cultural insularity can no longer be sustained in the face of the twentieth-century's experience of two catastrophic world wars and the prospect of a third. That poetry must inevitably take into account a new consciousness of global interdependence, and that it must also come to terms with the burgeoning sciences of psychology and psychoanalysis which have identified in external events manifestations of similar forces at work within each of us. Alvarez concludes with an illustrative comparison between Larkin's 'At Grass' from *The Less Deceived* and Ted Hughes's poem, 'A Dream of Horses'. It must be stressed that the essay does not essentially mount an attack on Larkin. In fact, in some respects, it is quite complimentary to him, acknowledging that 'At Grass' is 'elegant and unpretentious and rather beautiful in its gentle way'. What Alvarez insists upon, however, is that poetry should now go beyond the gentility principle, take risks, and proclaim an 'urgent' engagement, as Hughes in his poem, with its 'powerful complex of emotions and sensations'. If poetry were to combine the technical skill and formal achievements of a T. S. Eliot with the psychological insight of a novelist like Lawrence it would, argues Alvarez, result in a kind of seamless Coleridgean weld of emotion and order, accurately reflecting a post-Freudian world which has rendered the late Romantic dichotomy between emotion and intelligence totally meaningless.

Although Alvarez's essay reads persuasively, it tends to over simplify and in consequence seriously misrepresents Larkin, especially when it is considered in the light of almost fifty subsequent years of scholarship devoted to him. Larkin's technical ability, his highly developed sense of form and structure is undeniable. Although in his Introduction to *All What Jazz* he notoriously set his face against Modernism, it is clear from the poetry, as John Osborne has pointed out, that in terms of his influence on Larkin's verse construction, metrics and content, T. S. Eliot had major significance for him.[1] Larkin also virtually worshipped Lawrence, as any reading in the early letters in Thwaite's edition will reveal. 'We draw strength and life from Lawrence's work,'[2] he writes, placing him above the Bible in terms of the kind of importance his message assumes. And although Alvarez seemingly dismisses Larkin's work as devoid of the psychological dimension he requires in the new poetry, Larkin had in fact a serious interest in the Jungian psychologist, John Layard, whose seminars he attended during his Oxford years. He tells Sutton that he has started to keep a record of his dreams (almost '95' of them),[3] and poems written from his earliest years such as 'Deep Analysis'[4] to 'Love Again,'[5] in the twilight of his creativity, reflect his familiarity with the realms of the subconscious. It is ironic in fact that Alvarez, without, of course, access to material that has since come to light, should have chosen Ted Hughes's 'A Dream of Horses' to point up a contrastive 'gentility' in Larkin's 'At Grass'. Dream 43, in the unpublished 'Record of Dreams', and discussed by Stephen Cooper,[6] reveals, in an actual dream about horses recorded by Larkin, an incontrovertible source for 'At Grass', depicting precisely that tension between formal restraint and natural Lawrentian power which is advocated by Alvarez in his essay. Furthermore, as Stephen Regan points out, for Alvarez to ascribe a new poetry of mental disintegration to the trauma of two world wars, or even because of them, to advocate a new seriousness in poetry is misleading if it fails to see that Movement poetry, and Larkin's in particular, is no less a product of wartime England than the urgent psychological pressures he identifies as a reflection of modern culture.[7]

  With the publication of *The Whitsun Weddings* and *High Windows*

---

1   Osborne, John, *Larkin, Ideology and Critical Violence: A Case of Wrongful Conviction* (Basingstoke: Palgrave Macmillan, 2008), pp. 57–63, 174–76, 234–36.....
2   *SL* 50.
3   *SL* 53.
4   *CP* 4.
5   *CP* 215.
6   Cooper, Stephen, *Philip Larkin: Subversive Writer* (Brighton: Sussex Academic Press, 2004), pp. 139–40.
7   Regan, Stephen, *Philip Larkin* (Basingstoke: Macmillan, 1992) p.30.

in 1964 and 1974 respectively, Larkin's reputation developed to the point where it was more or less assumed that he would inherit the title of Poet Laureate on the death of the then incumbent, John Betjeman. Both collections sold well and attracted mainly favourable reviews. Of *The Whitsun Weddings* Christopher Ricks had remarked that it represented 'the best poet England now has',[1] and there was therefore a degree of surprise when, twenty years later, Larkin declined the offer of the laureateship. By this stage, however, he was in uncertain health with only a year left to live, and he had not produced a further collection since *High Windows* ten years previously. *High Windows* had included some poems which, for the first time, struck a different note from those which had come to seem representative of his more usual voice, one which the American poet, Robert Lowell, had described as combining, like George Herbert's, 'elegance and homeliness'. Clive James, in his review of the collection in *Encounter* spoke of Larkin's obscurity in two of the poems, 'Livings II'[2] and 'Sympathy in White Major',[3] remarking that 'while wanting to be just the reverse, Larkin can on occasion be a difficult poet.'[4] The question therefore of development in Larkin's poetry can be provoked by such criticism which seems to indicate, by this time, a shift away from the kind of representational objectivity, lucidity and accessibility traditionally associated with the poetry, to a more oblique, perhaps overtly symbolist, technique. Larkin himself did not necessarily regard development as a virtue in a poet: 'Oscar Wilde said that only mediocrities developed. I just don't know. I don't think I want to change, just to become better at what I am.'[5] However, in *The Listener* eight years later he said,

> What I should like to do is to write different kinds of poem that might be by different people. Someone said once that the great thing is not to be different from other people but to be different from yourself'.[6]

1   *New York Review of Books*, 15 January 1965
2   *CP* 187.
3   *CP* 168.
4   James, Clive, *Encounter*, June, 1974, Vol.XLII, No. 6, p.68
5   Hamilton, Ian, 'Four Conversations', *London Magazine*, Vol. IV, No. 6, November 1964, p.77.
6   'Out of the Air: Not like Larkin', *The Listener*, 17 August 1972, p. 209.

Roger Day believes that if by development is meant a revolution in thought, then Larkin did not develop as such. However, in terms of the emergence of new subject material and greater accomplishment, development can certainly be a helpful term.[1] The distinguished Larkin scholar, James Booth, in his Introduction to *Trouble at Willow Gables and Other Fictions* identifies in Larkin 'a neat mid-century division between a pre-1950 novelist and a post-1950 poet'.[2] However, Stephen Cooper, in his important book, *Philip Larkin: Subversive Writer*,[3] emphasises continuity in Larkin. He examines the whole range of Larkin's oeuvre, from his earliest poems and attempts at fiction, to reveal how, rather than consigning such work to the status of marginal experiments, it should be acknowledged for the centrality of its contribution, not only to our understanding of the mature poems, but also to our construction of a literary voice speaking variously through genres such as girls' school fiction, poetic prose, dramatised debate and verse drama. The function of this voice, insists Cooper, is to be at all times subversive, and his monograph demonstrates by way of response to those critics who 'insist on seeing Larkin as a pedlar of unsavoury right-wing thought,'[4] how, throughout his career, Larkin destabilised the very attitudes his detractors accuse him of purveying. Just as, Andrew Motion argues, 'Larkin did not simply swap Yeats for Hardy early in his career' rather identifying how 'much of his best work takes the form of a dialectic between the attitudes and qualities of his two mentors, [5] Cooper would argue that 'whatever the timing of Larkin's stylistic transition, and however it is identified' a desire to discriminate between early and late periods 'distracts from the strong thematic continuities which pervade all Larkin's writing.'[6]

Stephen Regan has identified 'negative criticism' of Larkin with what he calls 'the assumed "Englishness"' of his poetry. He describes

---

1   Day, Roger, *Larkin* (Milton Keynes: Open University Press, 1987), p. 82.
2   Booth, James, ed. *Trouble at Willow Gables and Other Fictions* (London: Faber, 2002) xli
3   Cooper, Stephen, *Philip Larkin: Subversive Writer* (Brighton: Sussex Academic Press, 2004).
4   Cooper, Stephen, *Philip Larkin: Subversive Writer* (Brighton: Sussex Academic Press, 2004)., p.119.
5   Motion, Andrew, *Philip Larkin* (London: Routledge, 1982), p.15.
6   Cooper, *Philip Larkin*, p.123.

how words such as 'philistine', 'parochial' and 'suburban' have discredited his work.[1] In 1957 Charles Tomlinson, he reminds readers, had referred to 'Larkin's "narrowness"' and to how, in his poetry, the English recognised '"their own abysmal urban landscapes"'[2] and their '"stepped-down version of human possibilities"'. Even Donald Davie, who defended Larkin in his *Thomas Hardy and British Poetry* (1973), a significant work in which Larkin is placed as the latest in a long line of poets who represent a true 'English' strain in verse, refers to a poetry of 'lowered sights and patiently diminished expectations.'[3] Regan's criticism of Davie's assessment is that it indiscriminately speaks for 'all England and for all social classes.'[4] With Regan's criticism in mind, we might think, for example, of Wilfred Owen's 'bugles calling for them from sad shires' in 'Anthem for Doomed Youth', an elegiac poem which tends to leave altogether out of consideration the fallen conscripts from a Barnsley or a Sunderland, who had no particular connection with what might be termed the stereotypically English 'shires' for which they were assumed to be fighting.

In the criticism of Tom Paulin the issue of Larkin's 'Englishness' takes on a harder political edge. In a review published in the *TLS* in 1990 [5] Paulin offers a postcolonial reading of Larkin, identifying behind his lyrical voice the pervasive theme of national decline. This, he argues, can be detected in an early poem, 'The March Past' (1951), about a military band, but which he believes is dealing at a more fundamental level with 'Astonishing remorse for things now ended' (19).[6] It is equally, though much less obviously detectable, in a near contemporary poem included in *The Less Deceived*, 'At Grass', where the retired racehorses become 'heroic ancestors—famous gen-

---

1   Regan, Stephen ed., *Philip Larkin* (Basingstoke: Palgrave Macmillan, 1997), p. 6.
2   Regan, Stephen ed., *Philip Larkin* (Basingstoke: Palgrave Macmillan, 1997), p. 7.
3   Davie, Donald, *Thomas Hardy and British Poetry* (London: Routledge and Kegan Paul, 1973), p.71.
4   Regan, Stephen, *Philip Larkin* (Basingstoke, Macmillan, 1992) p. 32.
5   Paulin, Tom, 'Into the Heart of Englishness', a review of Janice Rossen, *Philip Larkin: His Life's Work*, The Times Literary Supplement, 20–26 July 1990 in Regan ed., *Philip Larkin*, pp.160–177.
6   *CP* 55.

erals' who 'stand at ease', having made their contribution to a now faded imperial grandeur.[1] Similarly, in 'Afternoons',[2] the autumn leaves falling 'in ones and twos' (2) where 'Young mothers assemble / At swing and sandpit' (6–7) are, for Paulin, 'rather like colonies dropping out of the empire'.[3] In other words, Larkin's poetry enables him to issue public statements disguised as lyrical poetry and, in this sense, his 'Englishness' is revealed as a symptom of that typical national reluctance to display emotion which is detectable as discomfort with, or anger at, not only the personality his inheritance has saddled him with, but also his sense of failure, loss, the end of empire.

Larkin's distinguished contemporary and fellow poet, Seamus Heaney, calls him 'a poet indeed of a composed and tempered English nationalism' whose voice is 'the not untrue, not unkind voice of post-war England, where the cloth cap and the royal crown have both lost their potent symbolism'.[4] Richard Bradford points out that in such a remark there is a connection being made here here 'between England's national decline and sexual disappointment', both evident throughout Larkin's poetry, and he quotes Neil Corcoran's comment that 'Larkin's idea of England is as deeply and intimately wounded by such post-imperial withdrawals [sic] as some of the personae of his poems are wounded by sexual impotence.'[5]

In an essay adapted from a lecture entitled, 'Lyricism, Englishness and Postcoloniality' (1994), James Booth, rehearsing arguments first presented in his monograph, *Philip Larkin: Writer* (1992),[6] dismisses the kind of critical approach favoured by Tom Paulin. Larkin, he writes, 'is a poet, not a propagandist', a lyricist who writes not 'to conceal or mystify his own "real" ideological concerns, but in order to transcend them'.[7] He detects, therefore, 'a desperate ring' in Paulin's

---

1 In Regan ed., *Philip Larkin,* p.163.
2 *CP* 121.
3 In Regan ed., p.160.
4 Heaney, Seamus, *Preoccupations: Selected Prose, 1968–78* (London: Faber and Faber, 1980). p.167.
5 Corcoran, Neil, *English Poetry Since 1940* (London: Longman, 1993), p. 87 in Bradford, Richard, *First Boredom, Then Fear: The Life of Philip Larkin* (London: Peter Owen, 2005).
6 Booth, James, *Philip Larkin: Writer* (Hemel Hempstead: Harvester, 1992).
7 In Regan ed., *Philip Larkin,* p.195.

assertion that the leaves falling in ones and twos (in 'Afternoons') are 'a metaphor for a sense of diminished purpose and fading imperial power'. The young mothers who stand in the playground are simply, for Booth, working class women—'When did such people ever represent England's imperial glory?'[1] They are no more a metaphor for empire than are 'the worn out old horses in "At Grass", which Paulin ingeniously interprets as metaphorical "retired Generals"'. For Booth the lyric, aesthetic reading of Larkin must remain a more rewarding one than that 'requiring elucidation by an ideological inquisitor'. Thus, a poem such as 'Afternoons' is, for Booth, a lyrical treatment of the subject of time and the passing of time and, 'Intensely English though he was', Larkin's lyricism', he writes, 'is profoundly at odds with his nationalism'.

However Larkin's 'Englishness' might be defined, whether as nationalism, contentment with the ordinary, the parochial and the suburban, this element, seen by some to provide the main constituents of the poetry, has been the object of negative critical attention. In 1968, for example, Colin Falck remarked that 'There are no epiphanies in Larkin's poetry', that his ordinariness, although it confers 'a certain kind of humanity' needs to be transcended.[2] Anticipating Booth, Falck believes that the function of poetry is not simply to accept but to transform. Larkin himself referred to his acceptance of things, what he called 'my fundamentally passive attitude to poetry (and life too, I suppose)'. This, he believed, was part of his overall determination to be less deceived. Action, he stated, 'comes from desire, and we all know that desire comes from wanting something we haven't got, which may not make us any happier when we have it. On the other hand suffering—well, there is positively no deception about that. No one *imagines* their suffering'.[3] J. R. Watson, in his essay 'The Other Larkin' (1975) takes issue with Falck, and indeed with Larkin himself, in arguing that in fact his poetry 'celebrates the

---

1   In Regan ed., p.196.
2   Falck, Colin, 'Philip Larkin' in Hamilton, Ian, ed., *The Modern Poet: Essays from "The Review"* (Macdonald, 1968), pp.108–9.
3   Hartley, George, 'Nothing to be Said', in Thwaite, Anthony, ed. *Larkin at Sixty* (London: Faber, 1982), p. 88.

unexpressed, deeply felt longings for sacred time and sacred space'.[1] Thus, for Watson, 'desire' becomes very much a part of Larkin's transcendence. He observes in the poetry a progression from 'a poise, or a pose, to an exposure or an epiphany'. Stephen Regan points out, however, that since Watson's stimulating essay, it has become fashionable to emphasise the 'transcendent' element in Larkin's poetry as 'a way of contesting the rather dull and unexciting terms in which the early Larkin criticism was posited'. He believes, though, that what has been lost in consequence is 'a concern for the secular or "desacralized" context in which Larkin's poetry was written and in which it continues to be read'.[2]

In discounting a weary 'thematic' reading of Larkin which often concentrates on a 'monotonous range of topics' of so-called universal relevance, Regan points out that Larkin's poems are themselves the products of history and that matters of birth, love, age and death, although they obviously have enduring significance, are part of a changing history of ideas which must be understood in the context of different times. In his critique of David Timms's *Philip Larkin*, the first full-length book study of the poet,[3] Regan points out as 'shrewd' Timms's comment that in 'At Grass' Larkin employs horses as an image of an idyllic life because, 'we are able to imagine the ideal, but it is no longer within our expectations.' To do so, Timms writes, 'would be to enter into those modes of historical and sociological enquiry which are inimical to practical criticism'.[4]

In fact, to examine some of Larkin's prose is revealing in the context of what much criticism has assumed about his 'Englishness'. In a review of Cyril Connolly's *The Condemned Playground* in 1983, Larkin singles out from Connolly's diary extracts, *England Not My England* (1927–29), some of the latter's remarks on his native land—'Really, the most deplorable country [...] Women all dowdy, men undersized and weedy. Pathetic voices and gestures, newspaper-fed

---

1   Watson, J. R. 'The Other Larkin', *Critical Quarterly*, 17 (1975), pp. 347–60, 348, 354.

2   Regan, Stephen, *Philip Larkin* (Basingstoke: Macmillan, 1992), p. 33.

3   Timms, David, *Philip Larkin* (Edinburgh: Oliver & Boyd, 1973).

4   Timms quoted in Regan, Stephen, *Philip Larkin* (Basingstoke: Macmillan, 1992) p.38.

ignorance', all of which recalls for Larkin, 'at times', he says, his idol, D. H. Lawrence.[1] Larkin goes on to write that there is a study to be made of this literary hatred of England between the wars. 'Was it owing', he asks, 'to the rise in the cost of living? The emergence of the working class? The strict sexual climate and laws against homosexuality'. Here we see Larkin himself involved in precisely the kind of sociological enquiry demanded by Regan as necessary for a balanced and incisive criticism of his poetry. Twenty years previously, in a letter to Robert Conquest, Larkin had anticipated the opinions of Cyril Connolly: 'I am feeling a bit out of sympathy with England at present—God, what a hole, what witless crapulous people, delivered over gagged and bound to TV, motoring and Mackeson's stout!'[2]

One of the most important studies of Larkin to have appeared in recent times, John Osborne's *Larkin: Ideology and Critical Violence: A Case of Wrongful Conviction* (2008), takes as its point of departure the contextualisation called for by Stephen Regan and, among many issues, addresses the critical history of Larkin as 'A rootedly English Poet'.[3] Osborne argues that far from being rooted in England, Larkin's poems with their goings, comings, arrivals, departures,[4] are suggestive, instead, of deracination. He cites examples of poems, supposedly 'English' in theme, which are demonstrably uncertain of reference, while Larkin's readings in French, Irish and American literature make, as he demonstrates, the dominant Anglocentric interpretation of his oeuvre comically inept. In a critique of Larkin's 'I Remember, I Remember', Osborne points out that a poem supposedly about the poet's 'roots' has as its setting, Coventry, *through* which its speaker is travelling, and home appropriately to the Rootes Group motor industry which first made England's social mobility possible. He wittily remarks that Thom Gunn's poem about bikers, 'On the Move', a classic of Alvarez's 'New Poetry', presents its observer as static, whereas it is Larkin who is effectively a 'movement' poet in

1   *FR* 143.
2   *SL* 245.
3   Osborne, John, *Larkin, Ideology and Critical Violence: A Case of Wrongful Conviction* (Basingstoke: Palgrave Macmillan, 2008).
4   'Going' (*CP* 3), 'Going, Going' (*CP* 189), 'Coming' (*CP* 33), 'Arrival' (*CP*) 51, 'Arrivals, Departures' (*CP* 65), 'Poetry of Departures' (*CP*) 85.

the true sense of the word. When the same poems which led some critics in the 1950s to assume that Larkin was rootedly Irish, were later sometimes enlisted, and by the same critics, as proof that he was rootedly English, Osborne can only conclude that 'the poems are radically unhoused and that it is the critics themselves who assign them a national identity.'[1]

Osborne takes as the turning point in revisionary Larkin criticism Barbara Everett's essay, 'Philip Larkin: After Symbolism' (1980),[2] in which she not only points up Larkin's acquaintance and affinities with French poets such as Gautier and Mallarmé, but also demonstrates the extent to which he parodies symbolist techniques, thus in a sense identifying himself as a post-symbolist writer. In the process of contrasting Larkin (to his favour) with the arch-Modernist, T. S. Eliot, Kingsley Amis refers to Eliot's *The Waste Land* as a poem which, on its publication, represented for him a kind of club from which he felt he'd been excluded, with notes referring him to books he'd never read by writers he'd never heard of, and so on.[3] John Osborne points out, however, that Larkin is a notoriously unreliable source of information where his statements on literary and artistic affinities are concerned. Although he denounces Modernism, Larkin's extraordinary palimpsestic range and citationality are, according to Osborne, 'only explicable in relation to Modernist aesthetics', and he identifies echoes of Eliot in almost fifty of the poems.[4] Like Eliot, Larkin uses intertextuality but avoids a hierarchy of values in his allusive techniques. He thus 'effects a democratization of Modernist allusion and shifts literary practice towards a Postmodernist poetics'.[5] Here Osborne clearly aligns himself with Barbara Everett who refers to how Larkin, in viewing Modernism retrospectively, has produced poems which appear to have 'profited from a kind of heroic struggle *not* to be modernistic [...] they have wished to be, not merely

---

1   Osborne, 134.
2   Everett, Barbara, 'Philip Larkin: After Symbolism', *Essays in Criticism*, 30 (1980), pp.227–42.
3   *Poets on Poetry: Eliot and After* (BBCTV, 1988)
4   Osborne, p.56.
5   Osborne, p.79.

after, but well after Eliot'.[1] It is interesting to note that Eliot him-
self wrote approvingly about Larkin to Faber's editor, Charles
Monteith: 'Yes—he often makes words do what he wants. Certainly
worth encouraging'.[2] Stephen Cooper points out, too, the influence of
Virginia Woolf on Larkin, especially her novels, *To The Lighthouse*
and *The Waves*,[3] and also of James Joyce's 'After the Race' and 'The
Dead' (both from *Dubliners*) on Larkin's second novel, *A Girl In
Winter*, where Katherine's isolation, he writes, 'is experienced by
many protagonists of modernist fiction whose piecing together of
broken fragments conveys a greater sense of lived experience than
traditional realism'[4]

Richard Palmer, in a recent monograph devoted to Larkin's inter-
est in, and writings on, jazz music adds his voice to those who find
Larkin's pronouncements on the destructive tendencies of repre-
sentative Modernists ('Parker, Pound [...] Picasso')[5] misleading.
In a selection from the columns Larkin contributed to *The Daily
Telegraph* between 1961 and 1968, Palmer notes that 'All the musi-
cians cited (apart from Tatum and Webster) are modernist in persua-
sion, an aesthetic Larkin is supposed to have detested'.[6] Only in the
'Introduction' to *All What Jazz*, he writes, did Larkin 'seek to belit-
tle Parker'. Elsewhere 'he recognizes [him] as a force of nature'.
Of a comment by Larkin on Dizzy Gillespie, he writes, 'It is not
easy to see how [it] could be bettered, even by a Gillespie enthu-
siast.'[7] John Osborne acknowledges that there is a danger here that
'one absurdity (that Larkin owed nothing to Modernism)' might be
swopped for another '(that he owed everything to Modernism)'. The
point Osborne wishes to make, however, is that Larkin wrestled with
one after another of contemporary masters of the art of poetry, and

---

1 Everett , Barbara, *Philip Larkin: After Symbolism* in Regan, Stephen, ed.,
   (Basingstoke: Palgrave Macmillan, 1997), p. 58.
2 Quoted in Thwaite, Anthony, *Larkin at Sixty* (London: Faber, 1982.
3 Cooper, Stephen, *Philip Larkin: Subversive Writer* (Brighton: Sussex Academic
   Press, 2004), pp. 3–4.
4 Cooper, p.56.
5 'Introduction' to Larkin, *All What Jazz*.
6 Palmer, Richard, *Such Deliberate Disguises: The Art of Philip Larkin* (London:
   Continuum, 2008), p.17.
7 Palmer, p.38.

that his relation to Modernism must, in this light, be seen as 'evaluative and contestatory' rather than simply 'passive'.[1]

The basis of John Osborne's monograph is the emphasis it puts upon the need to avoid the misleading conclusions to which biographical readings of Larkin's poetry can often give rise. Stephen Regan in his critique of Simon Petch, *The Art of Philip Larkin* (1981)[2] notes its concern with Larkin's 'use of a speaker whose credibility varies from poem to poem,' seeing in this what he calls, 'a useful antidote to those biographical readings of the poems which fail to make any distinction between poet and persona and so evaluate the work in terms of what they imagine to be Larkin's personal lifestyle'.[3] Osborne's term for critics of this school is 'late millennial bowdlers'[4] who have imposed meanings and interpretations, often with farcical consequences, on what is 'known' about Larkin's life and personality. James Booth, on the other hand, in *Philip Larkin: The Poet's Plight* (2005), argues that some poems are not only enhanced by, but actually inextricable from, the poet's biography.[5] He quotes Robert Lowell's 'Memories of West Street and Lepke', from his *Life Studies* collection, as an example of the latter, whereas Larkin's 'Deep Analysis,'[6] although it reads, says Booth, perfectly well without a biographical placing, is nevertheless enhanced by being seen as one of what might be called his 'marriage debate' series of poems.[7] Osborne, whose stated primary objective is to 'revolutionize Larkin studies by 'releasing the poems from [a] hegemonic methodology', is concerned not to 'annihilate biographicalism', which has its uses, but simply to 'dislodge it from a monopoly position'.[8] In a survey of prominent critics who have commented on the title poem, 'The Whitsun Weddings', he shows how they have 'wittingly or unwittingly, raced, sexed, aged, classed and national-

---

1   Osborne, *Larkin, Ideology and Critical Violence*, p.60.
2   Petch, Simon, *The Art of Philip Larkin* (Sydney, 1981).
3   Regan, Stephen, *Philip Larkin* (Basingstoke: Macmillan, 1992), p. 40.
4   Thomas Bowdler (1754–1825) published an expurgated edition of Shakespeare and his name has become associated with censorship—to 'bowdlerise'.
5   Booth, James, *Philip Larkin: The Poet's Plight* (Basingstoke: Palgrave Macmillan, 2005), p. 48.....
6   *CP* 4.
7   Booth, p.58.
8   Osborne, p.25.

ized the narrator in accord with what they know about the author'.[1]

In Larkin's case, the relationship between the art and the life became an unavoidable issue on the publication in 1988 of Anthony Thwaite's edition of *Collected Poems* (revised in 1990). Thwaite's editorial policy was to depart from the carefully orchestrated collections which Larkin had produced in his lifetime, and replace them with a sequence of poems, including more than sixty post-1945 works which had remained unpublished, all in the order in which Larkin had written them, according to his own dating. Larkin himself had said that he took 'great care' in ordering the poems in a particular collection, treating them, he said, like a music-hall bill, 'you know, contrast, difference in length, the comic, the Irish tenor, bring on the girls'.[2] Thwaite's edition, however, revealed for the first time the processes and difficulties of poetic creation through periods of productivity and intervals of silence, reflecting, it would seem, events and various crises in the poet's own life. *Collected Poems* placed Larkin's first collection, *The North Ship*, together with work produced between 1938 and 1945, in a section at the end of the volume. In 2003, Faber brought out a new *Collected Poems*, again under Thwaite's editorship, but this time restoring the order of the four volumes of 1945, 1955, 1964 and 1974 as Larkin had published them, and putting into appendices thirty-five poems which had been published separately in magazines and newspapers. A succinct account of this publication history is to be found in Chapter One of James Booth's *Philip Larkin: The Poet's Plight*.

Prominent among the critics of the first *Collected Poems* (1988), and anticipating much more widespread and vociferous criticism on the publication in 1992 of Thwaite's edition of *Selected Letters* and Andrew Motion's authorised biography, *Philip Larkin: A Writer's Life* (1993), was Germaine Greer in her review in *The Guardian* (October, 1988). Greer identified a bullying voice in Larkin which seldom allowed to the reader 'any role other than complicity in what is being confided'. While his verse is 'deceptively simple, demotic, colloquial', she wrote, 'the attitudes it expresses are also anti-intel-

---

1   Osborne, p.64.
2   *FR* 55.

lectual, racist, sexist, and rotten with class-consciousness'.[1] Stephen Regan points out that very few critics at this time had explicitly condemned Larkin's verse in this way and that these were 'serious claims which made the earlier charges of "narrowness" and "parochialism" look very slight'.[2]

From here on, and through the 1990s, Larkin's personal reputation went into serious decline with an inevitable effect on the status of his work. The letters in particular, with their gibes against women, their explicit racism and their expressed loathing for many aspects of modern England's social democracy, led Tom Paulin in the *TLS* to describe them as a 'revolting compilation which imperfectly reveals and conceals the sewer under the national monument Larkin became'.[3] Lisa Jardine, as a prominent London University teacher, wrote in *The Guardian* in 1992 of Larkin's 'throwaway derogatory remarks about women', his 'arrogant disdain for those of different skin colour or nationality', and said that his poetry would no longer be taught as a set text in her English department. In feminist quarters in particular, Larkin's perceived attitudes met with dismissive opposition. According to Janice Rossen, 'a large part of Larkin's depiction of women has directly to do with violence against them'. She saw him as representative of 'a corporate group of men' and as speaking '*from* a deep subconscious level'. Writing about 'Deceptions' from *The Less Deceived*, she talks of its 'callousness' and 'sadism' and of how such writing ought to be seen as 'problematic' and 'as a limitation in Larkin's art'.[4]

The story goes on much in this mode, with further revelations about Larkin's somewhat seedy addiction to pornography, his various right-wing postures, and so on, providing ammunition to critical factions, cumulatively creating his popular reputation, in some quarters, as a fascist, racist, sexist, and socially marginalised figure. It could be argued that the now dead poet was, in Auden's terms, being

---

1   Greer, Germaine, 'A Very British Misery', *The Guardian*, 14 October 1988,), p. 27.

2   Regan, Stephen ed., *Philip Larkin* (Basingstoke: Macmillan, 1997), p. 4.

3   Paulin, Tom, Letter to *The Times Literary Supplement*, 6 November 1992, p.15.

4   Rossen, Janice, *Philip Larkin: His Life's Work* (Hemel Hempstead: Harvester, 1989), pp. 75, 89,90.

'punished' and 'modified' by the 'evidence' mounted up against him.[1]

Since the beginning of the new millennium, however, critical assessment has begun to take another turn as a much broader range of Larkin's work has become available. The *Collected Poems* in themselves proved Larkin to be a more prolific writer than the three celebrated slim collections seemed to indicate. James Booth's edition of the 'Brunette Coleman' works, the unfinished novels and other prose (2002), has made it possible to take a variety of new and different perspectives on the work. A. T. Tolley's edition, *Early Poems and Juvenilia* (2005) collected all the poems Larkin completed up to and including the compilation of his unpublished book, *In the Grip of Light*. Eventually, Faber will publish the Complete Poems of Larkin, currently work in progress under the editorship of Archie Burnett.[2]

Meanwhile, Steve Clark's essay '"The Lost Displays"': Larkin and Empire' describes 'a striking convergence between the apparently antithetical viewpoints of those who think Larkin should be banned [...] and those who concede the defects in the life, but separate the achievements of the poems from it.'[3] Among the latter must be included Alan Bennett who, in his review of Andrew Motion's biography in *The London Review of Books* entitled 'Alas! Deceived', regrets, he says, as though losing a friend, learning unpalatable truths about Larkin. 'Reading it I could not see how [the poems] would emerge unscathed', he writes, 'But I have read them again and they do'.[4] Prominent critics who have been carefully examining the actual evidence in Larkin's oeuvre have come to wholly different conclusions from those who represent the extremes of political correctness. Clive James, for example, finds it difficult to square Larkin's concern to build up the Labour Archive at Hull University's Brynmor Jones Library, with the popular perception of him as 'a rabid reactionary'.[5] Stephen Cooper writes that far from being 'politically *in*correct there

---

1   W. H. Auden, 'In Memory of W. B. Yeats'.

2   See Kelly, Terry, 'Larkin Revisited: An Interview with Archie Burnett', *About Larkin: Journal of The Philip Larkin Society*, No. 25 April 2008.

3   Clark, Steve, '"The Lost Displays"': Larkin and Empire' in Booth, James, ed., *New Larkins for Old* (Basingstoke: Macmillan, 2000), p.170.

4   Bennett, Alan, *The London Review of Books*, 25 March 1993.....

5   James, Clive, *Even as we Speak: New Essays, 1993-2000* (Basingstoke: Picador, 2001), pp.111–12.

is evidence to show that even in the 1940s Larkin was steadfastly opposed to misogyny and chauvinism,'[1] and that although he is frequently accused of being 'a rampant nationalist and a sexist bigot' he radically questioned, along with his friend Jim Sutton, 'settled assumptions—about the war, capitalism and gender issues.'[2]

Quoting a piece on black American history in his *Telegraph* jazz column of June 1963, in which Larkin appeals for advances in the civil rights of the Negro, and looks forward to a time when he is 'as well housed, educated and medically cared-for as the white man',[3] Richard Palmer writes of how such sentiments expose the 'post-Motion and post-*Letters* furore about his "racism" as the nonsense it is'. A true racist, he adds, 'would either be incapable of having such thoughts in the first place or wouldn't dream of proclaiming them so eloquently'.[4] Even Larkin's dabbling in the pornographic demi-monde, it might be said, pales into insignificance when seen in the context of material now freely available and seemingly acceptable on television, in cinema and on the internet. Equally, many of his expressed opinions that have been subsequently judged offensive were in fact widely shared on various aspects of contemporary culture and were by no means peculiar to him.

The most powerful defender to date of Larkin as victim of ideological critical 'violence' is John Osborne. It is not, he writes, 'a tolerable critical incompetence that plays into the hands of the zealots who show-trialed Larkin's works for moral misdemeanours of which they are entirely innocent. It is a scandal'.[5] The last chapter of his monograph which, taken as a whole, is a tour de force of Larkin criticism, demonstrates a lively twenty-first century resurgence of interest in the poet and outlines Larkin's extensive influence throughout a range of different art forms. Barbara Everett has said, 'There can be few other major poets who have been as often and as reasonably

---

1   Cooper, Stephen, *Philip Larkin: Subversive Writer* (Brighton: Sussex Academic Press, 2004), p. 89.
2   Cooper, p.94.
3   *AWJ* 87.
4   Palmer, Richard, *Such deliberate Disguises: The Art of Philip Larkin* (London: Continuum, 2008), p.66.
5   Osborne, *Larkin, Ideology and Critical Violence*, p.186.

called "minor" as Larkin has'.[1] All the signs now are that Larkin's status as one of the major voices, not only of the twentieth-century, but also in the canon of English literature, is well on the way to being consolidated.

---

1   Everett, Barbara, 'Philip Larkin: After Symbolism'.

Part 5 Bibliography

Larkin Texts and Biography:

Thwaite, Anthony, ed., *Philip Larkin: Collected Poems* (London: Faber, 1988).

Thwaite, Anthony, ed., *Selected Letters of Philip Larkin: 1940–1985* (London: Faber, 1992).

Philip Larkin: *Required Writing: Miscellaneous Pieces 1955–1982* (London: Faber, 1983).

Thwaite, Anthony, ed., *Philip Larkin: Further Requirements* (London: Faber, 2001).

Tolley, A. T. ed., *Philip Larkin: Early Poems and Juvenilia* (London: Faber, 2005).

Motion, Andrew, *Philip Larkin: A Writer's Life* (London: Faber, 1993). The standard life of Larkin by a friend and one-time colleague.

Selected Criticism

Booth, James, *Philip Larkin: Writer* (Hemel Hempstead: Harvester Wheatsheaf, 1992). Contains subtle readings of a range of the poems with a very good first chapter on Larkin's life.

Booth, James, *Philip Larkin: The Poet's Plight* (Basingstoke: Palgrave Macmillan, 2005). Examines the poetry from the point of view of Larkin's intense 'plighted' emotional commitment to his art.

Booth, James, ed., *New Larkins for Old* (Basingstoke: Macmillan, 2000). An important collection of essays by prominent Larkin scholars on topics such as Gender, Symbolism, Postmodernism and Post-Colonialism.

Bradford, Richard, *First Boredom, Then Fear: The Life of Philip*

Larkin (London: Peter Owen, 2005). A good recent critical biography.

Cooper, Stephen, *Philip Larkin: Subversive Writer* (Brighton: Sussex Academic Press, 2004). Argues that Larkin's work shows a subversive tendency from his earliest output. Contains interesting material on his debt to writers of the 1930s as well as the relationship between his work and that of his artist friend, Jim Sutton.

Osborne, John, *Larkin, Ideology and Critical Violence: A Case of Wrongful Conviction* (Basingstoke: Palgrave Macmillan, 2008). A major, recent work on Larkin which aims to refute the accusations which have damaged his reputation while providing illuminating readings. An excellent book with which to begin Larkin studies.

Palmer, Richard, *Such Deliberate Disguises: The Art of Philip Larkin* (London: Continuum, 2008). The first book to be devoted to a critical examination of the centrality of jazz in Larkin's life and work.

Regan, Stephen, *Philip Larkin* (Basingstoke, Macmillan, 1992). Argues that Larkin's work should be read historically and contextually, exposing the limitations of narrowly thematic and formalist criticism.

Regan, Stephen, ed., *Philip Larkin* (Basingstoke: Palgrave Macmillan, 1997). An important collection of essays by some of the most prominent Larkin scholars.

Tolley, A. T. *My Proper Ground: A Study of the Work of Philip Larkin and its Development* (Edinburgh: Edinburgh University Press, 1991). Particularly useful on the earlier work of Larkin.

Bibliography:

Bloomfield, B. C., *Philip Larkin: A Bibliography* (London: Faber, 1979).

Recordings

Listen presents Philip Larkin reading The Less Deceived (Listen LP, The Marvell Press, 1959)

Philip Larkin reads and comments on 'The Whitsun Weddings' (Listen LP, The Marvell Press, c.1965).

British Poets of Our Time. Philip Larkin: 'High Windows': Poems read by the Author (Arts Council of Great Britain, c.1975).

The Sunday Sessions: Philip Larkin Reading His Own Poetry (Faber CD, 2009). A discovery of readings of twenty-six poems, some from *The North Ship*, recorded by Larkin in Hull in February 1980 by John Weeks, a sound engineer and colleague of the poet, which had remained 'lost' on a shelf in a garage where they were recorded. They are here published in full for the first time.

Website

The Philip Larkin Society — http://www.philiplarkin.com — arranges events, meetings and conferences, and publishes a twice-yearly journal, *About Larkin*.

Appendices: Three Intertexts

William Blake: 'London'

I wander thro' each charter'd street,
Near where the charter'd Thames does flow,
And mark in every face I meet
Marks of weakness, marks of woe.

In every cry of every man,
In every Infant's cry of fear,
In every voice, in every ban,
The mind-forg'd manacles I hear.

How the Chimney-sweeper's cry
Every black'ning Church appals;
And the hapless Soldier's sigh
Runs in blood down Palace walls.

But most thro' midnight streets I hear
How the youthful Harlot's curse
Blasts the new-born infant's tear,
And blights with plagues the Marriage hearse.

William Shakespeare: 'Sonnet 116'

Let me not to the marriage of true minds
Admit impediments. Love is not love
Which alters when it alteration finds,
Or bends with the remover to remove:
O no! it is an ever-fixed mark
That looks on tempests and is never shaken;
It is the star to every wandering bark,
Whose worth's unknown, although his height be taken.
Love's not Time's fool, though rosy lips and cheeks
Within his bending sickle's compass come:
Love alters not with his brief hours and weeks,
But bears it out even to the edge of doom.
If this be error and upon me proved,
I never writ, nor no man ever loved.

From: John Keats: Ode on Grecian Urn, Lines 31–50

Who are these coming to the sacrifice?
  To what green altar, O mysterious priest,
Lead'st thou that heifer lowing at the skies,
  And all her silken flanks with garlands dressed?
What little town by river or sea shore,
  Or mountain-built with peaceful citadel,
    Is emptied of this folk, this pious morn?
And, little town, thy streets for evermore
  Will silent be; and not a soul to tell
    Why thou art desolate, can e'er return.

O Attic shape! Fair attitude! with brede
  Of marble men and maidens overwrought,
With forest branches and the trodden weed;
  Thou, silent form, dost tease us out of thought
As doth eternity. Cold Pastoral!
  When old age shall this generation waste,
    Thou shalt remain, in midst of other woe
Than ours, a friend to man, to whom thou say'st,
  "Beauty is truth, truth beauty"---that is all
    Ye know on earth, and all ye need to know.

Humanities Insights

These are some of the Insights available at:
http://www.humanities-ebooks.co.uk/

General Titles

An Introduction to Critical Theory
An Introduction to Rhetorical Terms
Modern Feminist Theory

Genre FictionSightlines

Octavia E Butler: *Xenogenesis / Lilith's Brood*
Reginald Hill: *On Beulah Height*
Ian McDonald: *Chaga / Evolution's Store*
Walter Mosley: *Devil in a Blue Dress*
Tamora Pierce: *The Immortals*

History Insights

Oliver Cromwell
The British Empire: Pomp, Power and Postcolonialism
The Holocaust: Events, Motives, Legacy*
Lenin's Revolution
Methodism and Society
The Risorgimento

Literature Insights

Jane Austen: *Emma*
Joseph Conrad: *The Secret Agent*
T S Eliot: 'The Love Song of J Alfred Prufrock' and *The Waste Land*
*English Renaissance Drama: Theatre and Theatres
in Shakespeare's Time*
William Faulkner: *The Sound and the Fury*
Elizabeth Gaskell, *Mary Barton*
Thomas Hardy: *Tess of the d'Urbervilles*
Josephh Heller: *Catch-22*
Hughes: *New Selected Poems*
Henrik Ibsen: *The Doll's House*
G M Hopkins: Selected Poems
D H Lawrence: Selected Short Stories
D H Lawrence: *Sons and Lovers*
D H Lawrence: *Women in Love*

Paul Scott: *The Raj Quartet*
William Shakespeare: *Hamlet**
William Shakespeare: *Henry IV*
William Shakespeare: *The Merchant of Venice*
William Shakespeare: *Richard II*
William Shakespeare: *Richard III*
William Shakespeare: *The Tempest*
William Shakespeare: *Troilus and Cressida*
P B Shelley: *Frankenstein*
William Wordsworth: *Lyrical Ballads**
Fields of Agony: English Poetry and the First World War

Philosophy Insights

American Pragmatism
Barthes
Thinking Ethically in Business
Contemporary Epistemology
Critical Thinking and Informal Logic
Ethics
Existentialism
Formal Logic
Metaethics Explored*
Contemporary Philosophy of Religion*
Philosophy of Sport
Plato
Wittgenstein

* also available in paperback

Also Available from *HEB*

Jared Curtis, ed.,
*The Poems of William Wordsworth:
Collected Reading Texts from the Cornell Wordsworth.*
3 volumes, ebook and paperback.

Colin Nicholson, *Fivefathers: Interviews with late Twentieth Century
Scottish Poets*

Keith Sagar, *D. H. Lawrence: Poet*
ebook and paperback

Ralph Thompson, *View from Mount Diablo*